LMS Challenge
2023-24

WHEN the WORLD
TURNED
UPSIDE DOWN

WHEN the WORLD TURNED UPSIDE DOWN

K. IBURA

SCHOLASTIC PRESS / NEW YORK

Library of Congress Cataloging-in-Publication Data available

ISBN 978-1-338-74626-6

10 9 8 7 6 5 4 3 2 1   21 22 23 24 25

Printed in Italy   183

First edition, November 2021

Book design by Keirsten Geise

TO MY DAUGHTER, WHO MET THE CHALLENGES OF
THE PANDEMIC WITH GRACE, VULNERABILITY,
AWARENESS, GRIT, AND PRAGMATISM.

SWEETIE, YOU ARE THE PERFECT
QUARANTINE PARTNER.

A NOTE FROM THE AUTHOR

Dear Reader,

The characters in this book are unique—as are you. They each have their own identities and their own voices—as do you. The world is a more beautiful place when we all express ourselves authentically and bring our own unique strengths and perspectives to our communities.

Let's work together to make sure the world hears our unique voices!

Yours,

K. Ibura

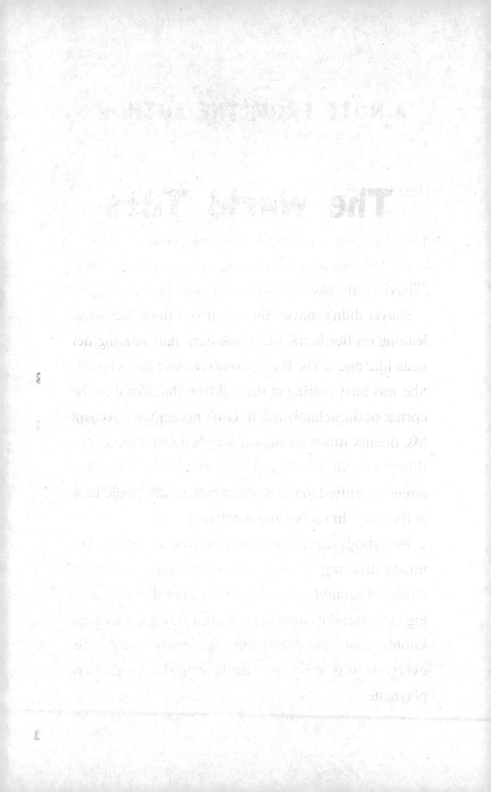

The World Tilts

"Shayla?" Ms. Breaux called. "Are you listening?"

Shayla didn't move. She sat at her desk, her head leaning on her hand, her thick dark hair haloing her head like one of the fluffy clouds outside the window. She was busy staring at the tall tree that stood in the corner of the schoolyard. It didn't matter what subject Ms. Breaux was teaching—if Shayla didn't have something to do with her hands, her mind drifted and her attention shifted to the window, where she would look at the tree's branches and daydream.

Everybody circled around the tree at recess. For ninety dizzying minutes, kids of all shapes and sizes clustered around it, leaning on its smooth bark, playing tag around its broad trunk, and sitting on its huge knobby roots. But during the long, lonely hours while everyone was in class, Shayla was the tree's only playmate.

On this morning, Shayla was imagining the tree's branches were sea creatures. The tiny bright green buds sprouting from the branches were the creature's scales and the tree trunk was a submarine diving down to the ocean floor.

Ms. Breaux called Shayla's name a third time, but she still didn't answer. A slap on her arm finally tore her away from her thoughts.

"Owww," she said, snapping her attention back to the classroom.

The room was completely quiet and Megan was smirking at her from the next seat over.

"Why'd you do that?" she whispered.

Megan didn't answer. Instead she tilted her head toward the front of the classroom. Ms. Breaux was looking at Shayla sharply and her classmates were staring at her silently like a bunch of wide-eyed frogs.

"Oh," Shayla said under her breath, suddenly realizing Ms. Breaux was waiting on an answer, but Shayla hadn't heard the question.

"She's asking about the book," Megan whispered.

Shayla sat up taller in her seat and looked at the colorful posters stuck to the walls as if they could magically reveal the answer to her. Just past Megan, she could see Gemma hiding her mouth behind her hands, her shoulders shaking with laughter.

"Ummmm, welllllllll, I thinnnnnnnk," Shayla said, slowly stretching every syllable and crossing her fingers under her desk for good luck. She was just about to launch into a rambling description of the chapter from last night's homework when the principal rushed into the room and dumped an armful of orange papers on Ms. Breaux's desk.

"One second, class," Ms. Breaux said, and Shayla slumped against the back of her chair in relief.

"Your participation grade is going to be horrible," Megan said as Ms. Breaux and the principal started whispering in the front of the room. She said the word *horrible* so hard Shayla felt like it had flown out of Megan's mouth and smacked into her cheek at top speed.

"She's never ready when Ms. B calls on her," Gemma threw in.

"Nobody asked you," Shayla snapped. She sank even deeper into her seat, wishing she could pull a tent over her desk. She peeked down at the sore spot on her arm where Megan had hit her. Her skin was stinging and it was slightly raised, but it was the same brown color as the rest of her skin. So different from the bright red mark that would be left behind if she had smacked Megan back.

"We're on chapter six," a soft voice whispered from the seat behind her.

Shayla swiveled around and found herself face-to-face with Ai.

"What?" Shayla whispered back. She hadn't even realized she was sitting there.

"I said we're talking about chapter six," Ai repeated. Then she flicked her finger up to point at Megan and Gemma. They were giggling together. "You think that's how friends are supposed to treat you?" she asked. Shayla shrugged, but she couldn't turn away. There was nothing mean in Ai's voice. She just looked at Shayla with a bucketload of sadness in her eyes.

Shayla sat there, trapped between the glare of Ai's honesty and the pull of Megan's and Gemma's friendship. Ai sighed into the emptiness of Shayla's silence.

"She wants you to explain why the main character left home at the end of the chapter. You did read, didn't you?"

The way Ai's eyebrows drew together made Shayla think Ai's question was about so much more than homework.

"I read, thanks," Shayla said, suddenly finding her words. She knew her response was short and sharp, but she didn't care. Why did Ai think she could decide who Shayla should be friends with?

She twisted back to the front of the classroom and straightened herself in her seat. She peeked over at Megan and Gemma. They were huddled together, talking and giggling as if Shayla wasn't even there. This was how it had been all year. Shayla didn't know how it had happened, but she was full of a fever that made her turn her back on Ai so she could hang out on the edge of Megan's and Gemma's friendship, trying to find a way in.

"Students," Ms. Breaux said, clapping her hands to call everyone's attention before Shayla could figure out what Megan and Gemma were talking about. Ms. Breaux held up the stack of papers the principal had brought in. From her seat, Shayla could see the words *School Closure* in big, bold letters across the top of the page. "As you know, we have been discussing how to continue safely teaching during this time. Some of your classmates are already learning from home and some of your parents are working from home. We have just received word that the governor has decided to close schools for the next two weeks."

"What?" Megan said. She looked at Shayla then. They were briefly connected in shock. Shayla turned back and looked at Ai.

Everyone started talking at once.

Ms. Breaux clapped again. She put both her hands in the air and held them there until everyone in class fell silent.

"We will communicate with your parents," she said softly and firmly. "We will send you assignments to complete at home." She looked at the clock on the wall, then walked to the doorway of the classroom. "You are dismissed. Please stop at the desk and pick up one of the announcements. Put these sheets in your folders immediately—and give them to your parents as soon as you get home."

Shayla stood up with the rest of the class, unfolding her long limbs from the small cramped chair.

"Megan," she called out, but Megan had already slipped away, rushing toward the front of the class-room with her arm tightly linked with Gemma's. Shayla darted out from behind her desk, but someone tugged her back. She turned to find Ai and Ben standing behind her.

"What?" Shayla asked, trying hard not to sound as grouchy as she felt. She felt like the tree in the yard, towering over Ai and Ben. She shifted her weight on her hip, which made her tower over them just a tiny bit less.

It wasn't that she didn't like Ai and Ben—it just felt like she couldn't get away from them. They all lived in the same apartment building. They had spent their toddler years in their friend Liam's apartment so Liam's mom could watch them while their parents worked. They spent the first years of elementary school hanging in the park together. And now Ai and Ben were in her class at school. Shayla had had enough. She wanted to try to make her own friends— at least one friend that her father didn't make for her.

"We have to find Liam," Ben said, irritated. He didn't like Shayla's new attitude.

"Why?" Shayla asked. She crossed her arms. It didn't matter what Ai and Ben thought. She had a right to be independent.

"How do you think he's taking this news?" Ai asked, circling her finger in the air.

Shayla's heart sank. She was instantly ashamed. She was so busy feeling trapped by Ai and Ben, she hadn't even thought about Liam. Change was not his friend. Once, when a substitute teacher showed up and announced he was replacing Liam's teacher for the rest of the school year, he shut himself in the supply closet and refused to come out. While they raced to call his mother, he tugged at his hair so hard he yanked out a patch the size of a dime.

With a serious nod, Shayla turned on her heel and headed over to the hooks. Reaching over everyone else's heads, she tugged down Ai's and Ben's bags. The three of them shrugged on their jackets and wrestled their backpack straps onto their shoulders. Just like that, every thought that was cluttering Shayla's brain fell away. Shayla forgot about wishing for new friends and sped out of the classroom, focusing on doing everything she could to get to Liam's side.

We'll Be Okay

Ai stood back and let Shayla yank open the door to Liam's classroom, but then she pushed past and hurried in first. They found Mr. Ogebi in the back of the room.

"He's in there, isn't he?" Ai said, startling Mr. Ogebi, who was kneeling in the doorway to the supply closet.

Ai was used to surprising people when she spoke. When she and Shayla would roam around the school together, it was Shayla who led the charge, asking the questions and starting conversations everywhere they went. People assumed Ai was shy or that she was afraid to talk, but she didn't mind talking—she just didn't like silly conversations.

"He's been in there ever since I announced school was closing," Mr. Ogebi said. He stood up and brushed the dust off his jeans.

"Benjamin," he said. "Could you go to the main office and ask Mrs. Jean to call Liam's parents?"

"His mom," Ben said, correcting Mr. Ogebi before rushing off to the office.

"Does he have his worry stones?" Ai asked.

Mr. Ogebi frowned. His face creased with concern. "I asked him about them, but he didn't answer me."

Ai stepped closer to the closet. "Can we try?" she asked.

Mr. Ogebi nodded. "Only because Liam's mother told me this might happen. She said the three of you knew how to help him calm down." He stepped to the side and swept his arm toward the closet.

"Ready?" Ai asked, nudging Shayla.

They stood shoulder-to-shoulder in the doorway of the closet, staring into the darkness inside.

"Liam?" Ai called out softly as she waited for her eyes to adjust.

There was no response, but every once in a while, they heard a soft sniffling sound break the quiet.

"Liam," Shayla said a little more loudly, "we're coming in."

By instinct, Ai reached for Shayla's hand, but she stopped herself. Instead, she held her hands out in front of her and stepped into the closet. Moving through the darkness side by side with Shayla almost felt like old times, but things had changed. These days Shayla acted like a stranger. She ignored Ai in class and sometimes didn't even say a word to her all day. No matter how much silence was between them, Ai's brain always remembered how things used to be, swooping back to the days when Shayla was friendly and funny, leaving Ai feeling like a Ping-Pong ball bouncing between the new Shayla and the girl who used to be her best friend.

As Ai and Shayla took tiny, hesitant steps in the dark closet, Mr. Ogebi opened the closet door wider. The light from the classroom cut a tiny sliver in the darkness, showing Ai a slice of Liam's pale cheeks and his dark red, curly hair.

"We're all going to get sick," he whispered.

It was the same thing he had been saying for weeks. Ever since the virus was announced on the news, Liam wouldn't quit talking about it. Every morning as they walked to school, he would repeat the latest from the news until he was breathless.

When they finally got close to Liam, they could hear how panicked he was. Every time he took a breath, it sounded like the air got stuck in his throat.

Then he would take a big gulp, gasping like he was desperate for air. The second Ai's foot collided with Liam's, she forgot about her friendship issues and grabbed Shayla's arm. She dragged Shayla down until they were kneeling in front of Liam.

They both frantically searched the air with their hands until they grabbed hold of Liam. Ai's hand landed on Liam's knee. She could tell from the bend of his legs that he was sitting curled over with his knees hiked up under his chin.

"Liam, you have to breathe," she said.

Liam took a deep breath and let it out. Ai could feel him shuddering under her hand, his whole body heaving like every breath was hurting him. It was terrifying, but not as frightening as it had been the first time Ai and Shayla had seen Liam have a panic attack. While they were playing at the park, they found him leaning over the fence with a red face, panting like he had been punched in the stomach. They had no idea what was happening to him. When he started struggling to talk, they grabbed him by the arms—one on either side of him—and rushed him out of the park. After the attack had passed, he described it like this: *It's like everything around you is fine, but your body doesn't know you are safe. Your body thinks you're in danger and it fills you up with fear.*

After learning what was happening to Liam, they had all invented their own ways of helping him. Even when they weren't sure what to do, they weren't afraid to try to help. The problem was, they were far away from Shayla's gadgets and Ai's art supplies. They were crammed together in a dark closet with nothing to distract Liam from his fears.

Ai's mind went into overdrive, thinking of everything that had worked before. Suddenly, she had an idea. She didn't hesitate. She didn't even warn Shayla. She just took a deep breath and started singing at the top of her voice.

"We got the whole world in our hands," she sang, chanting the first song that flashed into her mind. On the next line, Shayla joined in. They had all practiced it so many times for Parents' Night that it was burned in their brains.

Ai started gently tapping Liam in time with the beat. At first, Liam just sat there, still shaking and sputtering for breath. For a while, it seemed like Ai's idea had failed. Then out of nowhere, Ai heard Liam start whispering the word *world* each time it came around in the song. Ai couldn't see Shayla's face, but she could hear the excitement in Shayla's voice when she realized Liam was starting to sing in the breath between his gasps.

Ai and Shayla looped back to the beginning of the song, singing even louder. When they reached the chorus, Liam's voice got stronger too. By the time they started the song for the third time, they were all rocking back and forth together, belting out the words loudly.

Just when they were starting the fourth round, Mr. Ogebi leaned his head into the closet.

"Okay, Liam, are you ready to come out now?" he asked.

Ai held her breath while she waited for Liam to reply.

"I think so," Liam said after a long silence. His voice was shaky, but the gasping was gone and his breath was deeper and slower.

Relieved, Ai reached out in the dark and hugged him tightly.

"We're going to be okay," she said, pulling away from him.

Without warning, Shayla poked Ai in the arm. Ai didn't need to be friends with Shayla to know why Shayla had poked her. Shayla didn't believe in anything she couldn't touch with her own two hands. *How do you know?* was her favorite question. As they helped Liam to his feet, Ai knew what Shayla was thinking. They could not know what was going to happen in the future. Of course, Shayla was right. The truth was, no one could predict what was coming, so how could Ai know that they would all be okay?

Tiny Virus, Big Changes

After Liam's mom picked him up, Shayla, Ai, and Ben were stuck walking home together. *Stuck* wasn't quite the right word. Not for Ben. Walking home with Shayla was a treat since she didn't hang around them anymore. Before Shayla had abandoned them, Ben often found himself fighting to get a word in while Ai and Shayla shot rapid-fire conversation back and forth between them. But today was nothing like it used to be. Everything was uncomfortable as they walked past corner stores and apartment buildings in awkward silence.

Ben knew why Shayla and Ai weren't talking, but his silence had nothing to do with their friendship crisis—and everything to do with what was waiting for him at home. His stomach was knotted up with stress as he thought about his chart tracking his parents' fights. It had grown over the past few weeks since his dad's office closed because of the virus. The more time his dad spent at home, the more time his parents spent fighting. Then his mom's office closed two weeks ago and what used to be an argument once or twice a month had turned into a never-ending battle.

Now that both his parents were working from home, Ben had discovered degrees of fighting he hadn't known existed. His mom and dad could go from silence to nagging each other, to sharp criticisms that slid into all-out yelling. School had become an escape. So even though the news that school was closing down for two weeks didn't send him into a panic like it did Liam, it still filled him with dread.

The silence continued into the building, surrounding them as they trooped through the lobby and got into the elevator. The higher up the elevator went, the heavier the weight in his stomach grew. When they reached his floor, he barely mumbled goodbye as he stepped off the elevator. He trudged up to the front door, listening to the muffled sound of his parents' voices. He opened the door just in time to hear his mother wail, "I'm too far away from my family and I can't breathe in this city. I don't want to get stuck here."

"So leave," his dad shot back.

"Hi, Mama. Hi, Papa," he said softly. He dropped his backpack on the floor and let the door slam shut behind him.

"Oh, Benjamin." His mother sighed. "Your father didn't mean it."

Ben looked at his father. He almost didn't recognize him with the tense anger on his face. Everyone said they looked alike. Except for the tan skin color Ben got from his mother, Ben was like a smaller version of his father. They both had dark furious curls of hair, brown-rimmed glasses, and one-sided smiles. He kicked off his shoes, hoping he would never get so angry that he didn't recognize himself in the mirror.

Ben marched to his room without saying another word. The gray walls, blue curtains, and colorful animal posters were exactly as he'd left them, but somehow everything felt different. He switched on the light in Bucky's tank and peered through the glass to watch the turtle crawl across his log. Ben's mind flipped through observations as it always did. He noticed how healthy Bucky's shell looked, how Bucky was moving, and how much food was left in his bowl. But today he noticed something new. Bucky didn't have a lot of space inside the four glass walls of his tank, but Bucky was safe there. No viruses and no arguments. Ben sank into his desk chair and decided to hunker down in his room until his parents called him for dinner.

A few hours later, Ben's stomach started growling. It was five o'clock and he couldn't smell any food cooking. He went to the kitchen to investigate and found the stove empty. His parents were nowhere to be found. In the silence, he could hear urgent whispering spilling out from their room. With a sigh, he grabbed a bowl out of the cabinet and dumped cereal into it. After pouring milk in, he took his dinner to his room. Then he shut his door and sat down to eat, hoping to block out all evidence of his parents' disagreements.

●●●

The next morning, the first thing Ben thought about was getting out of the apartment. He could think of only one person who would be happy to see him that early in the morning. Tiptoeing around his room, he got dressed. Then he wrote a note to his parents and slipped out the front door. He took the stairs, running up two floors, and paused to catch his breath before ringing the bell at number 6C.

He was nervous as he waited at the door. After a

few minutes, the door opened and Shayla stood there, rubbing her eyes tiredly.

"What are you doing here?" she asked with a frown.

Ben poked his head in the doorway. "I'm here to help your dad."

Last month, Ben had run into Mr. Kwame in the lobby. When Ben helped him carry bags of fabric upstairs, he discovered that Shayla's living room was draped in fabric. Mr. Kwame had invited Ben to help him cut out patterns and he had spent hours cutting petal shapes out of shiny green fabric. This morning, he was surprised to find the living room was neat and tidy and the fabric was folded and piled in the corner. There was no shiny, sparkly, and satiny fabric hanging off the couch, puddling on the floor, or covering the dining table.

Ben shoved his hands in his pockets and stood awkwardly in the doorway, waiting for Shayla's dad to notice him. He hoped Mr. Kwame still needed help. When he didn't look up from his phone conversation, Shayla jerked her head and said, "Come in."

Ben stepped into Shayla's apartment hesitantly. He had left home to get away from uncomfortable changes, but things weren't quite normal at Shayla's apartment either. There were no fabric patterns lying around. No tinkling steel pan or bouncy reggae beat pouring from Mr. Kwame's speakers. And no big, booming greeting from Mr. Kwame as he said "Benjamiiiiiiiiiiiiiiiinnnnnnn Carloooooooooooooooos Christopherrrrrrrrrrrr" like a sports announcer.

Shayla left the living room and Ben followed her. She threw herself into the soft circle chair next to her bed and poked at a fluffy white rug with her toes. Ben wandered over to Shayla's dresser, trying to pretend that hanging out with her was completely normal. He picked up a ball that had lots of strings with tiny bells connected to it.

"What happened to all the fabric?" he asked, twisting the ball back and forth so that the bells rang out as he talked.

Shayla looked at Ben like she wanted to answer, but she didn't speak. Instead she covered her face with her hands. Her shoulders suddenly started shaking. Ben's eyes went wide when he realized she was crying. He had seen Shayla do lots of things, but he had never seen her cry.

"Are you okay?" he asked, peeking over at her.

Shayla wiped her face, then dropped her hands in her lap.

"They're all canceling!" she said.

"Canceling?" Ben asked, and dropped the ball on the dresser. "Why?"

Ben remembered how confused he had been the first time he discovered that Shayla's dad was a fashion designer—and that he worked from home. He thought all adults had jobs outside the house.

Shayla threw her arms up. "No prom!" she said.

"But . . ." Ben motioned to the living room and trailed off. Most of the work was already done. Mr. Kwame had already bought yards and yards of fabric, cut the panels to the right size, and sewn the base of the dresses. It was the magic moment when the fabric shapes transformed into dresses.

"I understand," Ben heard Mr. Kwame say from the living room. Then his voice got louder. "No refunds!" he said.

Ben suddenly felt angry. How could a virus—a tiny thing with no brain, no body, and no feelings—create so much chaos? At home, his parents were arguing about leaving New York City. At Shayla's house, her dad was fighting with customers about money. Things had to be normal somewhere.

"I'm going to the park," he said abruptly.

It was the farthest place Ben could think of from

his apartment, from Mr. Kwame, and from the whole building.

Shayla got up.

"I'm coming with you," she said, and disappeared into her bathroom. Ben's heart leapt. Shayla had pushed them away for so long. Her wanting to go to the park with him was like a little shock. Maybe the virus wasn't only bringing bad things. Yes, it was turning the world upside down, but maybe it could turn wrong things inside out. Maybe it could make Shayla stop acting like she forgot all the fun they used to have. Maybe it could make her be his friend again.

4

Time to Be Strong

Liam woke up to the sound of his sisters running up and down the hall, banging on the walls. He groaned. His mom wouldn't be back from her overnight shift for a few hours, so he was in charge.

He got up and made them wash their faces and brush their teeth. As soon as he sat them down for breakfast, Cara flipped her cereal bowl over, pretended it was a drum, and started tapping out a beat.

"I guess you don't want breakfast," Liam said.

He turned to Cayla's bowl, ready to dump cereal into it, but she covered her bowl with her hands.

"I want oatmeal," she said.

Cara grabbed her sister's bowl and started banging on the bottom of both. While Liam went to the cabinet for oatmeal, Cayla shoved Cara and grabbed her bowl back.

Liam returned to the table and poured Cayla's favorite flavor of instant oatmeal into the bowl.

"Cara, what do you want for breakfast?" Liam asked, taking the bowl to the sink and pouring water into it. He popped it into the microwave.

Cara squeezed her eyes shut and sang loudly, "OOOOOhhhhh, la, la, la, laaaaaaa."

Liam shrugged and brought the cereal boxes back to the cabinet. The microwave dinged and he brought Cayla's bowl to the table.

When she saw Cayla's breakfast, Cara slouched in her seat and crossed her arms with a pout. Cayla noisily blew on her oatmeal and slurped up a spoonful.

"I'm hungry!" Cara wailed.

Liam closed his eyes. This was obviously not a day that the twins could handle being cooped up inside the apartment.

Forty minutes later, both girls were fed and dressed. As they waited for the elevator, Liam explained how important it was for the girls not to touch the elevator buttons.

"Remember: Don't touch!" he yelled as his sisters went stampeding into the elevator. They wouldn't stop wiggling around and darting toward the railings and the buttons, so he made Cara put her hand in his right pocket and Cayla put her hand in his left pocket.

"Ooohhhh," Cayla said. "I got the pocket with the worry stones."

"Well, I have . . ." Cara paused as she dug deeper into Liam's pocket, searching to find something.

"Stop it," Liam said. "It's not a contest. I just need you to hold on to me."

Cayla stuck her tongue out at Cara. Then the elevator dinged and the doors opened on the bottom floor.

The girls dragged him forward as they rushed across the lobby.

When they got outside, Liam grabbed their hands. "Eyes forward. Feet focused on crossing the street. And don't let go. Okay?"

The girls fell silent, controlling their bodies as they crossed the street. But as soon as they made it to the sidewalk, the girls broke away and went racing into the park. He found a bench near the playground and watched the twins dangle from the monkey bars. In the park, the kids behaved exactly the same way they always did. They played tag, threw balls, and grabbed each other's arms as they ran around in circles. But Liam could feel the world shifting around him. It felt like the air was a ticking time bomb and he was the only one who could hear it.

He slipped his hand into his pocket and pulled out a mask. According to the news, no one needed to wear a mask if they weren't sick. In the videos from other countries, everyone had on masks, but Liam had never seen anyone wearing them in his neighborhood. It made him feel like no one was paying attention.

Liam looked around. No one was watching him. He put the mask on and practiced breathing with it. It wasn't so hard, but he could feel his breath, hot and moist, trapped in the mask and clinging to his skin. As Liam sat there, feeling the press of the mask on his face, Ben and Shayla went flying by on their skateboard and scooter so fast, he thought he imagined it. Embarrassed, Liam quickly snatched off the mask and stuffed it back in his pocket. They looped around the park, circling back to cruise to a stop in front of Liam.

"What was that?" Shayla asked.

"Good morning," Liam said back.

"You're rude," Ben said, nudging Shayla.

Shayla rolled her eyes. "Good morning," she said. "But what was that ... on your face?"

"A mask, obviously," Ben said, jumping in before Liam could answer.

"But why was he wearing it?" Shayla shot back. "He's not sick."

Ben wasn't like this with Liam, but with Shayla he always seemed to have something extra to say.

"I'm just trying to stay safe." Liam shrugged.

"Well, should we all get one?" Ben asked.

"That's what I've been wondering," Liam said.

"Where's Cara and Cayla?" Shayla asked.

Liam jerked his head toward the monkey bars.

"I'll be back," Shayla said, and glided away on her scooter.

After a few seconds of silence, Ben flipped his skateboard up and grabbed it in his hand.

"How's your . . ." Ben trailed off awkwardly. Ai and Shayla didn't seem bothered by Liam's panic attacks, but his anxiety seemed to make Ben nervous. ". . . your breathing," he finally said. "How's your breathing?"

"Good, so far," Liam said.

Ben flipped his skateboard onto its wheels and kicked it over to Liam.

"Wanna ride?" he asked.

Liam looked down at the worn skateboard. It

brought back memories of a time when he could go to the park without Cara and Cayla. It wasn't that long ago that he and Ben would grab their skateboards after school and go riding before they did their homework. But that time felt so far away.

Liam stood abruptly. Next thing he knew he was kicking and skating through the park. A soft breeze brushed against his body. Little by little, his muscles fell into relaxation and his thoughts started to slow down. He felt safe, like he was in his own little bubble and—as long as he was on the skateboard—the world couldn't touch him.

●●●

A week later, the world squeezed in a little tighter. School announced it would be closed for months instead of weeks and everyone would have to attend class on video. Even worse, when Liam and Ben met up at the park with both their boards, they found the black iron gates at the park entrance firmly closed. Inside the gates, the park was completely still—the tennis courts, the field of grass, the playground, and the trees were untouched. It looked like someone had zapped the park and made all the people disappear, leaving behind an empty green space.

Cayla and Cara grabbed the black bars and jerked

them back and forth, making the thick chain and padlock holding the gates together clang against each other.

"This is it, you know," Liam said.

"This is what?" Ben asked.

"The end of everything normal," Liam replied.

Ben went quiet. In the silence, Cayla yelled, "You're it," smacked Cara, and broke into a run.

As they chased each other down the sidewalk alongside the park, Liam felt the weight of sadness and fear swoop down to land heavy on his shoulders again.

"Let's find somewhere else to play," Ben said.

"I can't," Liam said with a sigh. "I'm stuck with them all day."

Then he took off after Cara and Cayla. As he ran, he felt the warmth of the sun on his skin and the wind brushing against his cheeks. He was in motion, but he felt trapped. Like the virus was right behind him, breathing on his back, and his sisters were forever in front of him, tripping, running, screaming, and crying. Like he had nowhere to hide and no time to rest.

Things Fall Apart

When Shayla woke up, she picked up the three magnetic balls that sat on her bedside table. She flipped them around with her fingers while her mind tumbled through ideas of how to help her father. In the past few weeks, she had tried baking his favorite dessert, cleaning her room, and making him a cheer-up card, but he always gave her that soft sad smile, kissed her cheek, and went back to moping around the apartment. She looked at her mother's photograph.

"What should I do, Mom?" she whispered.

She wished she could call her, but it was the middle of the night on the other side of the world where her mother lived.

Just as she was thinking about calling one of her uncles for help, she heard a sound she hadn't heard in a long time—the sewing machine! She sprang out of bed, pulled off her bonnet, and went to the living room. There was her dad, sitting in his sewing chair and hunching over the machine. It was a comforting sight, seeing his shoulders leaning forward and his long black locks tied back so he could work.

"Morning, Daddy," Shayla said, rubbing the back of her neck and looking around the room. All the shiny, sparkly fabric was still piled in the corner and a stack of bold and colorful African prints sat on the floor next to his chair.

"Morning, Sassy," her dad said without pausing the machine. Shayla broke into a smile. He was the only person that called her "Sassy" and it always made her feel warm inside.

"I thought no one was ordering dresses anymore."

"They're not," her dad replied. The machine never once stopped whirring.

"Soooooo . . ." Shayla went to stand next to her dad and watched the fabric run through the path of the stabbing needle. She was surprised to see half his face was covered from the bridge of his nose to his beard with a colorful mask.

"Soooooooo," her dad said. He finally paused the machine and looked over at Shayla. "I'm making masks. They're selling them everywhere. If I make a lot of them, I might be able to earn back some of the money we lost this season."

Shayla was quiet for a few seconds. She didn't know how much masks cost, but they would have to sell a lot of them to replace the money from prom dresses.

"And you're testing them out?" Shayla asked, tugging at the elastic strap around his ear.

"Yep," he said.

She saw his eyes crinkle with a smile.

"How do I look?" he asked, lifting his chin.

"You look like a boss," she said, giving him a fist bump. "Where's the pattern? Should I start cutting?"

"You can cut later. For now, you can grab a bunch of masks and deliver them to your friends," he said, pointing to a basket on the couch. Shayla looked inside and saw that it was full of masks. She turned to her dad in surprise.

"Did you sew all night?" she asked.

"I'm just doing my part," he said with a shrug. "Now go do yours before you have to get ready for school. Pick some out for your friends."

"But the sign says . . ." Shayla said, plunging her hand into the basketful of masks.

Her dad stopped sewing just as quickly as he had begun.

"They need to change that old sign downstairs. There's new rules."

"New rules that say I have to wear this?" Shayla picked up a mask and let it dangle from her fingers.

"Yes, to stop the virus from spreading. So you will wear one," he said, and started sewing again.

Shayla kept digging through the basket.

"And my friends? We barely see each other anymore."

"Ben's been over here twice already and you see Liam in the park all the time. And you know there's no way I'm going to be able to keep you and Ai apart."

Shayla felt a stabbing feeling in her chest. Her dad had no idea she and Ai weren't friends anymore.

"Masks aren't safe enough if only one person is wearing them. So whenever you're together, you're all wearing masks. Got it?"

Shayla nodded, but her mind was flying. Her father's voice faded into the background as she imagined the four of them walking through a busy hospital hallway, wearing masks and saving lives. When she finally snapped out of it, her dad was reaching his hand out to her with a long narrow strip of fabric hanging from his fingers.

"What's this?" she asked.

"Six feet. You have to keep six feet between you."

"So, this is like a tape measure?" She envisioned the green strip of plastic she loved to swipe from her father's sewing supplies to measure parts for her invented toys.

Her dad nodded. "Grab one end."

Shayla grabbed it.

"Now back up."

Shayla backed away until the fabric strip was pulled tight between them.

"That's six feet," he said.

"How are we supposed to play like that?" Shayla asked.

Her dad shrugged. "You're creative, you'll figure it out."

●●●

Bringing a mask to Ben and Liam would be easy, but showing up at Ai's door unexpectedly felt dangerous. Shayla could feel her heart thumping as she waited for Ai to answer. She knew she had started it when she had stopped hanging with Ai at school. But then Ai got her back by ignoring her in the building. Now everything between them was one big mess.

When Ai opened the door and saw Shayla standing there, her eyebrows went up in surprise, then they drew together in confusion.

"Hi," Shayla said. She was sure Ai was going to slam the door in her face, but then she realized Ai's face was sad, not mad.

"Are you okay?" Shayla asked.

Ai tried to talk, but instead she burst into tears. Shayla could hear her dad saying *Six feet!* in her mind, but she hoped a quick hug wouldn't hurt.

"What's wrong?" she asked after hugging Ai.

Ai wiped her face. For a few seconds, she just stared at Shayla as if she was deciding whether or not to talk. Finally, she let out a shaky breath.

"It's my mom," she said.

"What? Is she sick?" Shayla asked. She tried her best to keep her voice calm. Her emotions weren't going to help Ai.

"No, it's not like that," Ai said. Then she crossed her arms. "Wait! Why do you have on a mask? Are you sick?"

Shayla shook her head.

"My dad said we have to wear them now and . . ." She paused and looked at Ai awkwardly. Then she scrambled backward. "And stand six feet away from each other."

"Germs," Ai said, and nodded. "My dad wears his mask at the hospital all day. He comes home with marks on his face here and here." Ai pointed to each of her cheeks.

"So you already know about this? Everybody's supposed to wear them now." Shayla held out one of her dad's masks. "My dad made one for you too."

Shayla had picked one that was Ai's favorite color—a deep, dark indigo blue. Ai smiled when she saw it. But in the few seconds it took for her to reach out and grab the mask, the worried look returned.

"So, your mom?" Shayla asked.

"She's not sick. It's . . ." Ai looked down at her feet. "It's like a Liam thing."

"So, she had a panic attack?"

Ai shook her head no.

"She's been in bed for weeks. She won't leave her bedroom." Ai looked like she was going to burst into tears again, but then her father called her from inside the apartment.

"Yes, Ayah?" Ai said.

"You should be in the kitchen!" he yelled.

"The kitchen?" Shayla asked.

"I'm supposed to start lunch before class. I have to go," Ai said, and moved away from the door.

"But you don't . . ." Shayla was going to say that Ai

didn't know how to cook, but Ai shut the door before she could finish.

Shayla stood there for a few seconds, her mind busily trying to make sense of everything they had just talked about. The world might have turned upside down and they may not be friends anymore, but there was no way she was going to leave Ai to sort this out by herself. She stood taller and made a silent promise to find a way to help.

Friends to the Rescue

Ai piled an onion, a tomato, a head of garlic, and some lemongrass on the counter. Behind that she lined up two cans of coconut milk, kecap manis sauce, and shrimp paste. Then she put her hands on her hips and stared at it all. These were the seven things she always saw out whenever her mother cooked. She turned her head and stared down the hallway at the door to her sister Kartika's room. It was closed.

Kartika was the only person in the apartment besides her mother who knew how to cook a whole meal, but her father had told her she was absolutely not allowed to disturb Kartika right now. With midterms fast approaching, he refused to let the quarantine influence Kartika's grades. Ai sighed. She looked at the rice cooker on the counter, but she was afraid to use it. The one thing she was confident she could do was boil water.

She grabbed the rice from the cupboard. She found a saucepot in the cupboard, filled it halfway with water, and put it on the stove to boil. Then she took the chicken out of the refrigerator, sat it on the counter, and stared at it.

"It's you and me, chicken," she whispered under her breath.

Right when she was about to free the chicken from the plastic packaging, the doorbell rang. Ai rushed to the door and yanked it open.

"My dad is . . ." Ai was going to tell Shayla that her dad was sleeping and she couldn't ring the bell anymore, but she stopped short when she saw that there were two people outside her apartment: Ben and Shayla—both wearing masks—standing there on the opposite side of the door.

"Get your mask on," Shayla said. "We came to help."

Ai frowned. She felt a tug-of-war inside. On the one hand, she didn't want Shayla to think that anything had changed. Just because she'd cried in front of Shayla didn't mean she was going to invite her in— at least not until she knew she could trust her again.

On the other hand, she didn't want to go back to the kitchen to face the mysteries of cooking all by herself.

"What makes you think I would invite you in?" she asked with a glare.

"Come on, Ai," Shayla said. "Everybody knows you can't cook."

Ai's face darkened with annoyance.

"You can't cook either," Ai said.

"That's why he's here," Shayla said, jerking her head at Ben. "Let us in."

Ai stood in the doorway, not moving. The truth was her fight with Shayla wasn't the only reason she didn't want to let them in. She didn't want to show anyone how much her apartment had changed. It used to be full of family sounds, but now it had turned into a zombie house. Between her mother's depression, her father's exhaustion, and her sister's constant studying, the apartment was filled with a deadly silence.

"Ai," Shayla said, breaking into Ai's thoughts. "What do you have to cook?"

"Chicken," Ai said. "Chicken and rice."

"We can help you," Shayla said. "You can go back to ignoring me tomorrow."

"Fine," Ai huffed, "but we can't make a lot of noise or my dad will get upset."

"Your dad loves us," Shayla said.

"Right now, all my dad loves is sleep," Ai said, stepping aside.

"Let's do this," Shayla said. She flicked Ai's mask as she passed the hooks by the door. "Are you gonna put this on?"

Ai grabbed the mask and followed Shayla and Ben down the hall. Ai noticed Shayla was dragging a long string behind her. She couldn't help but grin. It reminded her of all the times she had helped Shayla think of ways to convince her father to buy her a pet. They had written him letters and made posters with lists of ways pets make people's lives better. They had even made a video. Mr. Kwame always encouraged their creativity, but he never changed his mind about pets. Whenever Shayla asked him why, he said he only needed one mouth to feed and one butt to wipe.

When they got to the kitchen, Ai said, "Shayla, did your dad finally buy you an imaginary pet?"

Ben laughed.

"Ha-ha," Shayla said.

Hanging out with Shayla was like one big

contradiction. No matter how mad Ai got, she couldn't turn off all the years they had been friends or all the memories. Whenever the memories came, she felt warm inside—then there was always a switch. She would remember that it was Shayla who had turned away from their friendship and thrown it in the trash. And just like that, all the good feelings would disappear.

"So why are you dragging around a bunch of fabric?" Ai asked, shaking off her thoughts.

"It's a safety tool."

"A tool?" Ai asked, her face scrunched in disbelief. Shayla was always coming up with fancy names for the simplest things. Shayla threw one end of the strip at Ai and held on to the other.

"You know we have to stay six feet apart, right?"

"And this is six feet?" Ai asked, holding up her end of the fabric strip.

"Wait," Shayla said. She walked out of the main area of the kitchen and circled around the counter. She reached over the countertop and said, "Hand me the strip."

Then she backed up. Ben watched as they stretched the fabric strip as far as they could.

"That," Shayla said, "is six feet."

Ai felt a chill go down her spine. Standing there in her kitchen connected to Shayla by the length of fabric, it felt like old times. She dropped the strip.

"Think fast," Ai said, and threw a tomato at Shayla. She hurled an onion at Ben right after.

Caught off guard, they both failed to catch the food. The tomato hit Shayla in the shoulder and the onion banged Ben on the forehead. Ai dissolved into chuckles, relieved to be laughing instead of thinking about her and Shayla's broken friendship.

"What was that for?" Ben asked, rubbing the spot where the onion had hit him.

"It's called safe food transfer," Ai said with a grin.

After that, Shayla and Ben caught Ai's silliness. Every moment of the cooking adventure felt like a never-ending joke. Somehow, the bad grains of rice that Shayla separated out from the good ones were cause for giggles. The way Ben poked at the puckered chicken skin made Ai laugh out loud.

After Ben talked Ai through seasoning the chicken and preparing the pot, Ai went quiet.

"What's wrong?" Ben asked.

"It isn't the right color," Ai said. Just because she didn't know how to cook didn't mean she wanted to feed her family food that didn't have the right seasoning. She lifted the cover off the rice. She got a nose full of the lemongrass and coconut scent. She put the top back on the rice and turned back to the pale chicken. She went over to the cabinet and pulled out all the seasonings she remembered her mother using—turmeric, ginger, and cumin. She sprinkled the chicken with seasoning, transforming its color with dark oranges and deep yellows.

"That's better," she said to herself.

Ai found herself smiling as she put the chicken in the oven. Nothing in her home was the way it was supposed to be. Children weren't supposed to be cooking while parents lay exhausted and depressed in bed. When her father had told her to make lunch, she had imagined nothing but disaster. She thought she'd end up cutting her fingers and spilling blood all over the food, or turning the oven too high and making the chicken explode. But in the end, it turned out that cooking wasn't a disaster after all. After feeling so alone, the sound of Shayla and Ben teasing each other behind her was just what she needed to shake off the day's blues.

Is the Neighbor Infected?

Ben left Ai's apartment with a big smile on his face. The smile stayed there after he'd said goodbye to Shayla and stepped into the stairwell to go back to his floor. It was the least awkward time he'd had with Shayla and Ai in what felt like ages. His grin turned into a chuckle as he replayed all the jokes and laughter. As much as he loved observation and measurement, there were some things a research study couldn't explain. It definitely couldn't explain why things changed.

Everything changed. Science taught Ben that. Even things that didn't move changed—the materials got weaker, the surfaces wore down over time, and you couldn't use them like you used to. In fact, that was exactly what Ben did with all his charts: He tracked changes. Some changes were more fun to track than others. The changes he loved to track the most were the things nobody noticed. The changes he hated tracking were the things that made him feel bad. Like losing his friendship with Shayla or his parents' fights.

Ben stepped out of the stairwell and paused as a realization hit him. All this time, he thought he was upset because people were changing—Shayla growing distant and his parents growing apart—but he realized he wasn't upset because they were changing; he was upset because their changes made him have to change too. His mind tried to organize the thought into a flowchart with arrows. Other people's changes change you.

Three months ago, this was exactly the kind of big thought he would discuss with his parents. He would get out his notebook and ask them a big question. Then they would debate—not the way they did now, with angry words, but with jokes and funny voices. They would each try to convince Ben that they had the best ideas. They would never give him one answer, and they always challenged him to find the answer that made the most sense to him. But their fights meant they stopped working together—and Ben had no one to turn to with his questions.

He dug his hands in his pockets and started walking toward his apartment, staring down at the toes of his sneakers.

"Pssst! Psst!" Ben's thoughts were interrupted by a hissing sound.

He looked around the hallway. Everything was still, but just a few feet behind him, Mrs. Connor's door was cracked open. Ben turned back.

"Mrs. Connor?"

He couldn't see anyone, but he could hear her dog whining. He crept toward her apartment.

"Mrs. Connor?" he said again, and stopped what he hoped was six feet away from her door. He had teased Shayla about her fabric strip, but he had to admit it would be great to know exactly how far six feet was right now.

Mrs. Connor didn't reply. Instead, she started to cough. Softly at first—and then harder and harder. Ben tensed up. He took three huge steps backward until he was pressed against the wall across from her door.

"Daisy is hungry," Mrs. Connor said after her coughing died down. "Do you have any dog food?"

Ben could hear her, but he couldn't see her. Just a strip of darkness where her door was cracked open. He shook his head. "I have a turtle."

"Oh," she said softly, then she went silent. In the background, Daisy's whining continued. Her screeching pitched higher and higher until it felt like an attack on Ben's ears.

"Is everything okay?" he asked.

Mrs. Connor peeked out, showing a sliver of face through the crack in the door. She looked pale and sweaty.

"Daisy really needs food," she said.

Ben gulped. Daisy's whining sounded panicked, and Mrs. Connor didn't look too good either.

"Do you want me to get you some? I . . . I can bring some tomorrow," Ben stammered.

"Yes. Thank you," she said with a huge sigh, and slowly closed the door.

For a few seconds, Ben was stuck standing there with his back pressed against the wall, listening to Mrs. Connor's coughs and Daisy's cries echo through the hallway, like an alarm, or a warning that more changes were sure to come.

●●●

One thing Ben had learned was that if he wasn't careful, his parents would use his words in their arguments. These days, the three of them spent dinner stiff and tense, as they worked hard to avoid falling into a fight.

Today, when Ben's father asked about school, Ben told him what they had learned about local farming and the activity they did to calculate their carbon footprint. His mom excitedly jumped in and started talking about her grandparents' farm. Ben opened his mouth to ask how many animals lived on the farm, but his father cleared his throat while his mother was still talking. He noticed that his father looked angry, so he decided he couldn't ask any questions about life on the farm. If he did, his father would think he was taking his mother's side, and that he wanted to leave the city too.

So instead of asking about the farm, Ben asked his father about his day at work. Even though his father was talking about things he loved—tagging and labeling cell images—his words were heavy with irritation and his face was tight with frustration. His mother stood up and Ben's heart sank. As soon as she started clearing the dishes from the table, he knew they were fighting without words.

After she noisily clattered the dishes in the sink, his mother returned to the table with caramel flan. For the first time in his life, Ben was disappointed to see dessert. Even though caramel flan was his favorite, he sped through it, shoving spoonfuls into his mouth as quickly as he could. He rambled about helping Ai cook in between gulps, then jumped up to get a head start on the dishes. As soon as he heard whispered hisses, he rushed to his room without another word to his parents.

He tried to start his schoolwork, but it was hard to focus. He looked at the novel he was reading for class. He flipped through his science notebook. He shuffled through his math worksheets. But his mind kept drifting. He started thinking about his parents, but then he thought of Mrs. Connor and Daisy. *Does she have a family?* he wondered. *Does she have the virus? Can I help Daisy?*

Leaning away from his desk, he snuck a glance into the hallway. It was empty. His parents were too busy arguing to check on him. He shoved his schoolwork to the edge of his desk and slid his laptop toward himself. "How do you know if you have the coronavirus?" he typed.

He started reading. At the end of the web page, he clicked another link. Wide-eyed, he read about the signs of the virus, how to stay safe, how long you would be sick, and what happens to you once you're sick. Then he clicked another link, and another. The web pages listed so many symptoms, he couldn't keep up with them. He leaned back and stared at the ceiling. As his mind sifted through the information he read, he realized three big things were repeated on every page: coughing, fever, and shortness of breath. He closed his eyes and tried to remember everything he heard and saw from outside Mrs. Connor's door. Mrs. Connor definitely had a cough, and she looked like she was sweating—maybe she had a fever. But it didn't sound like she was having trouble breathing.

Ben heard a thud echo through the hallway and sat straight up in his chair. He took a deep breath and listened. He didn't hear anything more, but it had to be his parents. He charged down the hall and stopped in front of their bedroom door. His heart started racing. He wasn't sure he wanted to know what was happening behind the closed door.

Suddenly, all he wanted to do was get far away from his parents. He rushed back to his room and went to his closet. Grabbing his robot bank from the top of his dresser, he pulled out two ten-dollar bills. He couldn't do anything about the virus raging outside and the fights erupting inside his apartment, but he could buy a few cans of dog food.

When he slammed his door shut, he heard the sound of his mother's music drifting through the apartment.

He knew that when he heard the sounds of the accordion and the Mexican singer wailing in Spanish, his parents' fight was over. He turned back to his laptop to look up dog breeds and dog food brands, letting his thoughts about his parents fade away as he got swept up in the research.

It's Scary Out There

Liam was in a battle with his brain. It was one thing to talk himself out of a panic attack when there was no real danger around him, but now that a virus, a tiny thing—tinier even than bacteria—was harming so many people, everyone had reason to panic. He worried about getting infected, but he tried to hide it from his mother. So even on a day when he was close to the edge, he did his best to follow his logic instead of his fears.

The day she came home from work, limped over to the couch, and fell against it in exhaustion before he could tell her there was nothing to cook for dinner, Liam knew what he had to do. He put on a brave face and told her he would do the shopping. After making the list, he went to his room and wrote down ten songs—ten songs he was sure he could sing from beginning to end, ten songs that could keep him company and help him stuff down any panic that might come up when he went out to face the world. Then he went back to the front of his apartment, careful not to let any worry show on his face. He put on his mask, checked his pockets for his worry stones, and waved goodbye to his mom.

The first song on his list took him all the way down the elevator, through the lobby, and onto the sidewalk outside. On his block, everything was quiet and there was nobody around. Before the virus, he would have heard kids playing in the park across the street, seen cars driving down the street, and had to dodge people with pets and carts on the sidewalk. In the silence, he felt free to sing out loud because no one was listening.

Halfway down the block, he stopped singing abruptly and squinted. He was sure that the two figures he saw walking ahead of him were Shayla and Ben.

"Hey!" he yelled, and started running forward, pushing his shopping cart as quickly as he could.

At the corner, Shayla and Ben turned back toward Liam. When he reached them, he was surprised to see they were wearing matching masks. Well, they didn't match exactly, but they were both made of brightly colored fabric with lots of patterns. Liam's was a boring blue and white.

"You have the same masks? Well, that's special!" he said. "Does Ai have one too?"

Shayla burst out laughing.

"Yes, she has one—and you do too, silly."

"Obviously, I don't!" Liam said, pointing to his nose.

"You do!" Shayla said. "Didn't Ben give it to you yesterday?"

Ben smacked his head and groaned.

"You forgot?" Shayla said.

"So I have one too?" Liam asked. His eyes narrowed like he was suspicious that Shayla was tricking him.

"Of course. My dad made one for all of us," Shayla said. "We're the . . ."

"Quartet," they all said together. It's what all the parents called them whenever they wanted to invite all the kids somewhere. But it didn't feel like they were a quartet these days. Besides the time Liam and Ben spent in the park, Liam barely saw any of them anymore.

Ben dug in his pocket, pulled out the mask, and held it out to Liam.

"Ewwww, you didn't change your pants," Shayla said.

"Actually, I did. I took the mask out of one pair of pants and put it in another. That's how pockets work."

Liam looked at the green-and-yellow pattern on this mask. Part of him wanted to put it on so it would feel like the Quartet was back together again, but another part of him didn't want to seem too excited. The cool part of him won, so he shoved the mask in his pocket and kept walking.

Before he knew it, they were approaching the grocery store. They were surprised to see a long line of people stretching down the block.

"A line?" Ben asked.

"To go to the grocery store?" Liam added.

Liam tightened his grip on the handles of the cart as they tried to find the end of the line.

"At least everybody's spaced out," Ben said.

Liam was happy to see the six-foot gaps between the people in line, but seeing so many people gathered together made him nervous. He kept his eyes straight ahead and started singing the second song from his list under his breath.

"Are you okay?" Shayla asked.

"Huh?" Liam asked. His muscles were tense and his palms were sweaty, but he thought that he was hiding his emotions. He was surprised that Shayla had noticed anything.

"I mean, there's a lot of people out here," Shayla said, swerving her cart around so they could join the end of the line.

Liam paused his singing and turned his cart around too. He noticed they were standing next to the entrance of a small courtyard. It had a few benches, some bushes, and a few tall trees—but no people. He made a note of it, just in case he needed to escape.

He started pushing his cart back and forth, listening to the wheels squeak. He felt shaky but stable. Usually, when panic was going to take over, his mind would catch hold of a scary idea and send it looping around in his thoughts again and again. It would balloon out and grow bigger and bigger, adding on scarier and scarier things until his fears were all he could think about. He couldn't see, he couldn't move, and he couldn't think, because the scary thoughts were taking up so much space in his body.

Suddenly, he heard Ben say, "Owwwww."

Liam snapped out of his thoughts. Ben was holding

on to the brick wall next to him and hopping on one foot.

"Ugh, you're so dramatic," Shayla said. "It barely touched your foot."

"Look," Ben said, pointing at his shoe. "You can see the wheel mark right there."

"Did I do that?" Liam asked.

As Shayla and Ben bickered, Liam felt his stress ease just a little bit.

"What are you doing here anyway?" Liam said to Ben, jumping into the teasing.

"Me?" Ben asked.

"Yeah, your mom buys all the groceries. You don't even have a cart."

"It'd be pretty dumb to bring a cart for a few cans of dog food."

"Dog food?" Liam's mind latched onto those two words. He was relieved to push away the worries that were circling his brain and focus on the mystery of why Ben needed dog food. "You don't have a dog."

"Oh," Shayla said. "Ben didn't tell you about that either?"

As Ben launched into the story, Liam kept a smile plastered on his face. Ai's apartment. Mrs. Connor's dog. Maybe there still was a Quartet—and he just wasn't a part of it. The three of them were having all kinds of adventures without him.

"No one invited me to Ai's apartment," he said.

Shayla and Ben stumbled over each other to explain how they ended up at Ai's apartment without him.

"You're always busy," Shayla said.

"And the twins are loud," Ben threw in.

"I like them," Shayla shot back.

"And it was right in the middle of the day," Ben added.

Liam's face was blank, but his mind was in overdrive. As annoyed as he felt to be left out, the hot rush of irritation and sadness helped keep him grounded in the world around him. His panic was like a train that—if it found a way through his boundaries—came barreling at him hard and fast. As much as it hurt to hear stories that left him out, the feeling of being abandoned was much easier to manage than a panic attack.

Being mad at his friends wasn't on his panic therapy list, but he was surprised at how well frustration and annoyance distracted him from his fears. He frowned. It turned out that there wasn't enough space in his mind for his friends' antics and the panic. As they moved closer to the front of the line, he had something new to think about. He had his worry stones and his songs, his therapist and his mom—maybe there were even more things he could do, more than he ever imagined, to keep his life settled and his mind calm.

We Have to Do Something

Shayla didn't miss the things about school that she thought she would miss. She thought it would hurt not to have a chance to finally figure out what to do to become one of Megan's crew, but it didn't hurt at all. She felt relieved. She missed running wild at recess, playing ball with the boys, returning to class with scraped knees and her hair loose and tangled. But she didn't miss the complex role-playing games that Megan and Gemma liked to play where lies and mean truths were all tangled up.

She had spent so much time trying to escape the Quartet. She had known them for so long that she could only see how they irritated her, how their friendship fit too tight. She wanted so badly to explode into newness that she had forgotten what comfort felt like, what history felt like, what home felt like.

She forced herself to focus on the computer screen. Ms. Breaux was talking about ecosystems and her whiteboard was covered with the names of different plants and animals. Ms. Breaux had drawn arrows between the words to show how everything was connected. Shayla's mind started churning when she heard Ms. Breaux say the biggest predator on the food chain couldn't survive without the help of the tiniest prey—the little bugs that frogs and birds eat. But this time her imagination didn't pull her away from Ms. Breaux's words. She listened closely as Ms. Breaux talked about how everything in life was connected, how everything was a system that needed all its parts working to function properly—the planets, the cells of the body, animals and ecosystems. Shayla was struck with a thought that made her sit very still. She realized that if the Quartet was an ecosystem, she would be the part that wasn't working.

As soon as class was over, Shayla jumped up and sent her chair clattering to the floor. She rushed into the kitchen and grabbed a knife out of the drawer.

"Sassy!" her dad yelled.

When she didn't answer, she heard his sewing machine pause.

"Shayla Marks, you better come in here and pick up that chair up."

Shayla wasn't ignoring her father—not exactly. She was just focused on pulling the cover off the pound cake he had baked over the weekend.

"Oh, now I know you have lost your mind," her father said.

Shayla jumped. His voice was right behind her, but she hadn't heard him come into the kitchen.

"It's not for me, Daddy. It's for Ai," Shayla said, as if that explained everything.

Her father crossed his arms, blinked his eyes, and waited.

"You see . . ." Shayla said, and launched into an explanation involving ecosystems and predators, recess and friendship.

"I only caught half of that, but it sounds like you're saying you've been a bad friend."

Shayla twisted her mouth to one side and nodded as she wrapped the cake in foil.

"So, can I go . . . bring it over to her?"

"After you pick up your chair and shut down the laptop," he said with a nod of his head. And when she brushed past him, he squeezed her shoulder.

"I'm proud of you. Anytime you do wrong, the best thing to do is find a way to make it right."

●●●

Ai answered the door barefoot with a paintbrush in her hand. She listened with a blank expression as Shayla breathlessly explained that she had been wrong. When Shayla was done talking, Ai nodded toward the plastic bag in Shayla's hand.

"Is that your dad's pound cake?" she asked.

Shayla scrunched up her face.

"Did you hear what I said?" she asked.

"Is it for me?" Ai asked, ignoring Shayla's question.

Shayla sighed and held the bag of cake out to Ai.

Ai snatched the bag and turned to go.

"Wait!" Shayla said. In a long rush of words, she told Ai all about Mrs. Connor and Daisy. When Shayla finished her story, Ai's eyes were sparkling. Her blank expression was gone.

"So, did you bring the dog food yet?" she asked.

"No. We're going now."

"I'm coming," Ai said, and disappeared into her apartment, leaving Shayla completely confused about what to do next.

Ai wasn't any more talkative on the way to

Mrs. Connor's. When they passed the window next to the stairwell, Shayla looked over at Ai, but Ai kept her eyes straight ahead. That spot was their spot—the halfway point between their two apartments. They had measured the distance in footsteps years ago, after Shayla's seventh birthday party. It started when Shayla had walked Ai to her apartment after the party, hyped up on excitement and sugary sweets. On the way, they made up a rap song. Then they walked back to Shayla's, making up a dance routine to go with their rap. At some point, after they had drifted back and forth between their apartments singing and playing games, they declared that they would find out the exact middle point between their apartments. After discovering that the window next to the stairwell was the halfway point, they had collapsed there, exhausted after roaming the hallways. An hour later, when Shayla didn't come home, her dad found the two of them, slumped against the wall, sleepily playing hand games. He took both of them firmly by the hand and delivered Ai to her parents, then gave Shayla a piggy-back ride home.

Since then, they had never passed that window without sharing a look. Shayla reached out and tapped Ai's elbow. She wasn't sure if she was supposed to do that with the virus rules, but she didn't care.

"So what do you think?" she asked. "About my apology."

Ai kept staring straight ahead.

"I'm not here for you," she said. "I'm here for Daisy."

Behind them, the door to the stairwell creaked open and Ben stepped out.

"Perfect timing," Ai said, and cut a look at Shayla.

"Oh, hey, Ai," he said. Then he turned to Shayla. He had a tray of dog food in his hands.

"I hope it's not too late?" Ben said. He looked worried.

"For Daisy?" Shayla asked. "You mean she could be . . ."

They all started walking a little faster.

"It's not too late," Ai said when they stopped in front of Mrs. Connor's door. "It can't be!"

Ben took a deep breath and rang the bell. After a few seconds of silence, he knocked.

"Wait, do you hear that?" Shayla asked, and she pressed her ear to the door. "I think I hear her." She was sure she heard Daisy whining, whimpering softly—like she was too weak to make a louder sound.

"We have to do something," Shayla said. Her voice was heavy with worry.

Ben moved away and Ai leaned her ear against the door. Reaching down, she grabbed the doorknob. Then she gasped.

"It's open," she whispered.

Shayla and Ben watched as she twisted the doorknob and cracked the door open. She froze, and looked at Shayla and Ben over her shoulder.

"What should we do?" she asked, her hand still on the doorknob.

"Let's just leave the dog food," Ben said.

"Mrs. Connor," he called as Ai backed away from the door. He knelt down, placed the cans of food on the floor, and pushed them into the apartment. Then he pulled the door shut. The three of them looked at one another.

Shayla shook her head. "We can't leave it," she said. "It's not going to work."

"Why not?" Ai asked.

"We have to open the cans."

"Why can't Mrs. Connor do it?" Ben asked.

"She might not even be there. Not if she's sick like you said," Shayla replied. She darted forward, pushed the door open, and scooped up the dog food cans.

"We can open them at my apartment," Ai said.

Shayla started to follow Ai down the hall.

"Wait!" Ben said.

Shayla and Ai turned to look at him.

"Are you serious? Are we really going in there?" he asked.

Shayla snuck a peek at Ai and saw that she had a determined look on her face—a look that told her that Ai wouldn't be convinced to ignore Daisy.

"What will happen to Daisy if we don't?" she asked.

"We can tell our parents," Ben said. "Or call 911."

Ai shook her head. "What do you think will happen to Daisy, then?"

"They'll send her to a shelter," Ben said softly.

"So we go in," Shayla said. "We go in, we feed Daisy, and we get out."

"Then we're going to need more than these masks," he said. The three of them fell silent.

As Shayla followed Ai back to Ai's apartment, her father's face flashed in her mind. She knew he would want her to be safe, but she couldn't let Daisy starve. If Mrs. Connor couldn't feed Daisy, then they both were in deep trouble—and Shayla felt like she had no choice. She had to help.

A Close Call

Ai dug through the kitchen drawer, wondering if she was doing the right thing. This was the second time she was hanging out with Shayla in one week. It would be so easy to slide back into her friendship with Shayla. But what if Shayla had apologized to her because they were all trapped in the building together and she had no one else to hang with? Ai didn't want a pretend friendship. She didn't want to fix things just to watch things fall apart all over again once school reopened.

She grabbed the can opener and went back to the hallway. Swiping the can out of Shayla's hands, she turned away to hide what she was doing. She bumped the opener to the top of the can. Nothing happened. She twisted the can opener and clinked it against the can. Still nothing.

Shayla reached around Ai and snatched the can back.

"Let me hold it for you," she said.

Ai frowned and grasped the can opener with both hands while Shayla held it in place. It was easier with Shayla's help, but instead of thanking Shayla, Ai avoided catching her eyes. She stared at the can and tried everything she could think of—she wiggled the can opener, flipped it, then squeezed it, but still nothing happened.

"I don't think that's how it works," Shayla said. "Let me try."

They switched jobs and Ai watched Shayla go through the same struggles with the can opener. When she started tapping it against the top of the can, Kartika poked her head out of the door. Her dark hair was piled high on her head and her glasses were tucked behind her ears. She looked annoyed.

"I should have known it was you two out here. Why are you so noisy?"

Before they could respond, Kartika saw how Shayla was holding the can opener and burst out laughing. "Who taught you how to use a can opener?"

"So you come all the way out here to make fun of us?" Ai asked.

"I came out here to see who was making noise in the hallway," Kartika shot back.

"Oh, sorry, didn't mean to disturb your precious studying."

Ai expected Kartika to snap back, but instead she locked eyes with Ai and stared at her softly. In those seconds, Ai felt the fullness of everything that had changed swim between them. If things were normal, Kartika would have been rude, but now that her father was always working and her mother had locked herself away, it seemed like Kartika had lost her spark.

"If I help you," she said, "will the two of you go somewhere else?"

"Yep, you'll have all the quiet you need," Ai said, making her voice sugary-sweet.

"Hold the can," Kartika said. She took the opener from Shayla and made a big show of opening it and clasping the round blade to the top of the can. She squeezed the arms until the blade broke through the metal with a pop.

"Oh!" Shayla said.

Ai and Shayla watched with fascination as Kartika turned the handle and the blade cut through the metal top. When Kartika was done, Shayla took the opener back. While she was examining the blade and handle, Ai snatched the opener out of her hand.

"Can you stop thinking about gadgets for a second? We don't have time for this," she snapped, and handed the opener to Kartika.

Ai pretended not to see the hurt expression on Shayla's face and led the way back to Mrs. Connor's. Ben was waiting there with masks and gloves. He handed the masks to the girls.

"Let's double up," he said.

Ai looked at Ben skeptically as she put the new mask on top of the mask she was already wearing. Then he handed them each a pair of blue plastic gloves.

"Ready?" Shayla asked when everyone had pulled on a pair of gloves.

Ai nodded and Ben pushed Mrs. Connor's front door open. Ai looked at Shayla, silently trying to figure out which one of them should step in first. When Ai noticed Shayla tilt forward, she darted ahead and stepped in ahead of everyone else. Shayla and Ben walked in behind her and let the door slide shut. In an instant, all the light was sucked out of the air. A strong odor surrounded them, making Ai hunch in the hallway, clutching the open tin of dog food in her hands.

In that moment, Daisy whimpered.

"Daisy!" Shayla said, and moved past Ai. Light coming from deeper in the apartment showed Ai a shadow of Shayla's body drifting down the hallway.

"Let's go," Ben whispered. Ai stepped forward, groaning "Owwww" under her breath when she banged into a shelf that jutted out from the wall.

Shayla was already crouching on the floor, rubbing Daisy's fur, when Ai made it to the kitchen. Ai flicked on the light switch and gasped. Daisy—curled against the bottom of the cabinets—didn't seem to have much energy to do anything more than wag her tail hopefully. That's when she saw a row of empty dog food cans lined up on the counter. Daisy's water bowl was lying on the other side of her, bone-dry. How many days had Daisy lain there, starving and terrified? Ai felt sadness pressing against her chest.

Daisy let out a desperate yelp and Shayla leapt into action. She stood and filled Daisy's water bowl in the kitchen sink, then knelt again, holding the bowl close to Daisy's face. For a few tense seconds, Ai held her breath as Shayla urged Daisy to drink. When Daisy finally started lapping up the water, Ai let out a sigh of relief.

Once Daisy lifted her head for herself, Shayla

placed the water bowl on the floor, patted Daisy on the head, and backed away.

"Bring the food," Shayla said.

But before Ai could move, she heard a rustling coming from the hallway. She shoved the can of food at Ben. She waited for Ben to approach Daisy with the food, then she slipped away. She was halfway down the hall when she heard Shayla whisper, "Ai, come back!"

"I just want to see if she needs help," Ai whispered, tiptoeing farther down the hall.

"You're not a doctor," Shayla whispered back, but Ai didn't stop. The second she heard the rustling, her mind latched on the need to check on Mrs. Connor. Everything else—all sound and thought of safety—faded away.

Just enough light filtered into the hallway to reveal the photographs in fancy frames covering the walls. There were black-and-white, old-timey baby pictures, brownish photos with people in old-fashioned clothing, colorful school photos and family group photos with kids who looked like they were her age. *With all these people in Mrs. Connor's life,* Ai thought, *how is it possible that no one knew that she was sick?*

Ai heard a loud outburst of coughing coming from a

room at the end of the hall. A streak of fear swept through her, but she couldn't turn away. Her need to know if Mrs. Connor was in trouble was stronger than her fright.

She crept to the doorway and slowly peeked inside. The room was dark, but a part in the middle of the curtains let a spear of light shine through. Ai took a tiny step forward and felt a crinkling underfoot. She looked down and saw towels and frozen food bags scattered across the floor. Deeper into the room, there was a bucket next to the bed. Ai squinted at the bed and saw a mess of rumpled blankets and sheets spilling off the side of the mattress. The sheets moved and Ai backed up. Mrs. Conner rolled over and leaned over the side of the bed as a fit of coughing sounded out and shook her body.

Mrs. Connor's coughing stopped as suddenly as it began. She caught her breath and looked up at the doorway. When their eyes met, Mrs. Connor stared at Ai for a few seconds. Ai stared back, wide-eyed, as Mrs. Connor shook her head as if trying to clear it. The hair around her face was wet and stringy and stuck to her skin. Her nightgown was dark with sweat.

"Mrs. Connor?" Ai said.

Mrs. Connor opened her mouth to speak, but another coughing fit grabbed hold of her.

Suddenly, Ai felt Shayla and Ben grabbing her from both sides and pulling her away from Mrs. Connor's bedroom.

"She really is sick," Ai said softly, like she couldn't believe it was true. Her mind was spiraling through all the things they could do. They could tell the super, bring more food for Daisy, call 911, find her family, but none of her thoughts formed into words.

We have to help, she wanted to scream, but her brain felt completely disconnected from her ability to speak. All she could do was follow her friends as they swept her out of the apartment, with Mrs. Connor's coughing echoing in her thoughts long after they had left the sick neighborhood behind.

This Is an Emergency

Ben stood outside his front door and squeezed his hands together. Ringing the doorbell was the last thing he wanted to do. What he really wanted to do was teleport himself to his room and hide under the covers. But seeing Ai standing in the hallway while Mrs. Connor was having a coughing fit just a few feet away wasn't really something Ben could hide. He wasn't sure what his parents would think, but he knew that Mrs. Connor needed help—and they couldn't do it alone.

He looked back at Ai and Shayla, then pressed the bell. When his mom pulled the door open, confusion swept over her face.

"Ben?" she said. When she saw Ai and Shayla behind him, she flashed them a warm, welcoming smile.

"Wait," she said, closing the door. She reappeared wearing a mask.

"Mama, we have to call 911," Ben said.

Her shoulders got tense and she ran her eyes over Ben's face and body.

"Who's hurt?" she asked, looking Ai and Shayla over.

"It's not for us," Shayla piped in.

"It's Mrs. Connor," Ai added.

When his mom looked at him again, Ben knew he'd better talk fast. He launched into the story, starting with Mrs. Connor asking for the dog food. His mom's face got more and more red as he explained how they went into Mrs. Connor's apartment and found Daisy. When he got to the part about hearing Mrs. Connor coughing in her bedroom, her eyes bugged out and she grabbed both sides of her head like it was about to explode.

"Abel!" she yelled.

Ben's dad stepped into the open doorway and Ben was struck silent with fear.

"Well," his mom said. "Tell your papa what you just told me."

Ben glanced back at Shayla and Ai. There was nothing but warning in their eyes. He hadn't mentioned that Ai had gone deeper into the apartment and forced him and Shayla to drag her out. Their faces told him he had better be careful about what he said. He launched into the story again. This time, he talked slower and chose words that made everything sound more safe and reasonable. But it didn't matter how softly he spoke. His dad's face tightened into the same shocked expression his mom's had.

"Get in the apartment," his father snapped.

Ben flushed with embarrassment. He felt heat on the back of his neck where he imagined Shayla and Ai were staring at him.

"Bye," he muttered, peeking at the girls over his shoulder before stepping into the apartment. Ben held his breath as he passed, hoping his father wouldn't say another word in front of Ai and Shayla.

"I'm disappointed in all three of you," Ben heard his mom say.

"We just wanted to help," Ai said.

"How much help would you be if you got the virus and infected your families?" his mom replied.

"But we were—" Ben wanted to say that they were safe, but before he got the word *safe* out, his mother cut him off midsentence.

"Inside," she snapped, then she turned back to Ben's dad. "I'm taking the girls home. I will let their parents know that they have been exposed." Then she pushed her feet into a pair of slippers and charged out of the apartment. Without being asked, Shayla and Ai turned on their heels and followed.

When they had walked a few feet away, Ben's father slammed the door shut and whirled around to stare at Ben. After a while, Ben's eyes wandered away from his father and he stared at the shelf of Mexican pottery his mother brought back home every time they took a trip to south Texas to visit his grandparents. As he waited, tense and worried about what his father would say, he looked at the bowls and plates and animals his mother had collected.

Ben held himself perfectly still, waiting for his father to blink. After what felt like forever, his father let out a sigh and rubbed the sides of his forehead.

"I'm racking my brain trying to figure out what you were thinking," he said.

"Daisy sounded like she was in trouble. We didn't want anything bad to happen to her."

His dad held his hands out. "A dog!" he said, lifting one hand. "Your life!" he said, lifting the other hand.

"A dog," he repeated. "Me and Mama's life!" He see-sawed his hands back and forth over and over again.

Ben hung his head down. His father didn't understand. He didn't even get a chance to tell him about the double masks and the gloves. And what about Mrs. Connor? They got her a Christmas card every year and always helped her with her groceries. When she asked for help, what was he supposed to do?

Ben peeked up to see that his father was no longer staring at him. He was pacing from the front door to the living room and then back again. Ben stood perfectly still as his father walked back and forth, muttering under his breath about tests, ambulances, and quarantine. Then, with a motion so sudden Ben felt the air brush across his cheek, his father charged out of the room.

Ben didn't move. When his dad rushed back into the room with his phone in his hand, he was still standing in the some spot. His legs were starting to ache, but he didn't dare walk away from his father, so he shifted his weight from one foot to the other as his father dialed 911 and pressed the phone to his ear.

He jiggled his legs as he listened to his father explain that a neighbor was sick with COVID-19. After sharing Mrs. Connor's apartment number, his father had no other details to offer. He stared at Ben as he said "I don't know" over and over.

Just when Ben felt like his knees were going to buckle, his father said "I understand" and clicked the phone off.

Ben tensed up, expecting his father to yell, but instead, he just reached down and squeezed Ben's shoulder.

"Do you understand how serious this disease is?" His voice was angry but calm.

"Yes," Ben said.

"You hear the sirens every night? The ambulances?" he asked. Ben nodded.

"Are you tracking them?"

Ben nodded again. He had created a chart in his notebook for tracking the number of ambulance sirens he'd heard since the beginning of the quarantine. When he started, he may have heard the ambulance once every few days. In the past week, though, he had heard sirens two or three times per night.

"And what do your observations tell you?" his father asked.

"That more people are getting sick?" Ben said. He ended his sentence like a question instead of a statement. He was confident about his research, but he was trying to make sure he said whatever his father wanted to hear.

"And if we are not careful—" Ben's father leaned even closer and poked Ben softly in the chest. "If *you* are not careful, one of us will be next. Is that what you want?"

Ben shook his head. The idea of him or his parents being rushed to the hospital in one of those ambulances stabbed him in the chest. As his father hovered over him, his face warmed and he felt tears struggling to break through his calm. Ben's dad held him by the chin and looked deeply into his eyes.

"Are you trying to bring the virus home to me and your mama?"

Ben pulled his chin away from his father's fingers and shook his head. The tears felt even closer to the surface.

His father straightened up and crossed his arms.

"Go to your room and write down why it was irresponsible of you and your friends to go into Mrs. Connor's apartment, then write an apology to me and your mother."

Ben rushed out of the room, relieved to be able to walk away before his tears spilled over. As soon as he left the living room, they broke the surface. By the time he got to his room, tears were streaming down his face. He threw himself onto his bed and pressed his face into the pillow, trying to hide the sound of his wailing.

In the middle of his crying, he heard a muffled clattering coming from outside. He wiped his cheeks and went to his window. When he opened it, he heard the neighbors cheering and clapping. His father came to his room. His face wasn't as angry and his energy was calmer. Without a word, he handed a spoon and pot to Ben, then rested his hand on Ben's shoulder. Together, they joined voices with their neighbors to thank all the people in the hospitals and the ambulances who were taking care of people with the virus.

When the cheering was done, Ben heard the front door open. His father pointed to his desk and left the room to talk to his mother. He sat down at his desk. He didn't want to think about his family getting sick— and he didn't want to think about it being his fault. He heard his parents talking in low voices. Guilt punched him in the chest. It was bad enough that he had probably gotten Shayla and Ai in trouble, but he knew that if his parents started fighting, that would be one more thing he ruined today.

He stared at the family picture that sat on his desk.

It was taken three years ago, so he was smaller. He was standing in his grandparents' yard underneath a tiger piñata with a big stick in his hand. He was surrounded by cousins on both sides of him. His grandparents stood behind him. They each had a hand on his shoulder as if they wanted to keep him close. To the right of his grandparents were his aunts and uncles; to the left were his parents. They had their arms around each other and they were laughing. Looking at the photograph, Ben was sure that all the fighting between his parents wasn't the way it was supposed to be. They belonged together, and maybe, somehow, if he didn't cause any more trouble, they could get along again. He took a deep shaky breath, then he grabbed a few blank sheets of loose-leaf paper, gripped his pencil tightly, and started to write.

Does Everyone Need Help?

Liam was surprised to hear the doorbell ring right in the middle of the girls' bath time.

On his way to answer it, he peeked at the couch. His mom was leaning on the armrest and she was fast asleep.

He was even more surprised when he opened the door and saw Ai standing there alone.

"I have to show you something," Ai said, motioning frantically. "Come with me."

"Shhh," Liam said, glancing at his mom. "You want me to come out? Right now?"

"You have to see this," Ai said, pressing her hands into a prayer. "Please. It won't take long."

Ai looked so hopeful. He didn't want to disappoint her.

"I need shoes!" he said, pointing to his feet. "And time to get the twins out of the tub."

Ai jumped up and down like she was about to burst. "I'll meet you in the trash room."

"The trash room?"

Ai nodded, as if meeting in the trash room was the most normal thing in the world.

"I'll be waiting," she said. "I can't go home until you meet me."

"Okay," Liam said. "I'll be there soon."

He closed the door and went over to the couch.

"Ma, Ma," he whispered.

She blinked a few times, then looked at him.

"I fell asleep?" she asked.

Liam nodded. She worked so hard on her shifts, but no matter how exhausted she was, there always was more to do when she got home.

"Ma, the girls are getting out of the tub. I have to help Ai with her homework. I'm going to go study with her, okay?" Liam said softly.

"Wear a mask," his mother mumbled sleepily, and closed her eyes again.

He shook her a little harder.

"I'm going to send the girls to you," Liam said. He pointed to himself and to the front of the apartment.

"I'm leaving. The girls are going to need pajamas. Are you up?"

His mother nodded and slowly stood.

"I'm up," she said. "You're sending the girls. I'll put them to bed."

Then she ruffled his hair and smiled at him. "Have fun with Ai. Don't stay out too long. And wear a mask."

Liam nodded and rushed back to the bathroom. He pulled the plug out of the tub.

"Up, up, up!" he said, clapping his hands. He grabbed the mermaid bucket from the corner and splashed the girls, washing off the bubbles.

In a blur of legs and arms, towels and giggles, he dried them off and sent them to their room. Then he looked for his gloves and mask so he could go find out what Ai was so excited about.

●●●

When Liam opened the door to the trash room, Ai yelled "Wait! Wait! Wait!" and pushed the door closed.

Liam tried to poke his head in, but Ai held the door closed.

"Back away!" she yelled.

Liam moved back until he was leaning against the

opposite wall. A few seconds later, Ai popped her head out. When she saw that Liam was far away from the door, she slipped out of the trash room.

"You ready?" she asked.

"So now you're going to let me in?" he replied.

Ai shrugged. "It's a small room," she said, walking away from the door. "I just wanted to be safe."

"So can I go in now?" Liam asked.

Ai slid a few feet away from the trash room and stood by the opposite wall. Then she motioned toward the room with a few wiggles of her fingers.

The moment Liam stepped into the trash room, a fluffy bundle of energy rushed toward his feet. Liam knelt.

"You're hiding a dog in here?" he yelled as he started petting a tiny gray terrier with curly fur.

Then he realized Ai couldn't hear him. He scooped the dog up and opened the door.

"You're hiding a dog! Wait, isn't this Mrs. Connor's dog?" Daisy's tail wagged furiously as Liam held her tight and rubbed her fur.

"Isn't she cute?" Ai said, clapping her hands. "I need you to help me figure out what to do with her."

"What do you mean, what to do with her? She's not your dog!"

"Well, I knew the ambulance was coming to pick up Mrs. Connor . . ." Ai's voice trailed off.

"Wait," Liam said. He put Daisy down. Gripping her leash, he looked across the hallway at Ai.

"An ambulance came? To pick up Mrs. Connor?" His eyes darted back and forth as he thought about what that meant. "So Mrs. Connor is sick . . . with COVID. And the virus—it's in the building?"

Ai looked puzzled. "I guess so." She shrugged.

Daisy yipped. Liam looked down at her and stared into her eyes. He looked at his hands. Suddenly, he felt itchy. What if Daisy had COVID stuck in her fur?

"So Daisy might have it too?"

Ai shrugged again. "Maybe, but I read that pets can't really give it to people."

"Are you sure?" Liam said.

Ai nodded, but Liam didn't believe her. His mind went spinning as Ai described everything that had happened that afternoon. He had gloves on, but did he touch his face after he petted Daisy? He was sure he didn't. Did Daisy lick his face? No, he assured himself, not that either. He started making a plan for when he got home. He'd change his clothes, wash his hands and his arms with antibacterial soap, and rinse out his eyes with eye drops.

"So you're going to quarantine?" Liam said. His words came out more forcefully than he usually talked. "And get tested?"

"Of course, and I'm going to stay far away from anyone until I get home. See?" she said, pointing to the space between them. "I just need help with Daisy. I can't take her home."

Liam's mind felt like it was going to explode as he thought about all the red flags that popped up in Ai's story.

"So why did you tell Mrs. Connor you could take her if you can't take care of her?" he finally asked.

Ai shook her head sharply. "I didn't. She doesn't know I have her."

"So you stole her?" Liam was so shocked that he swept his arms out, tugging Daisy along with the leash. "Sorry," he said to the dog. Then he looked back at Ai. "You took the dog?!"

Ai looked worried for the first time since Liam met up with her outside the trash room.

"I knew the ambulance was coming and I was afraid what would happen to Daisy if no one was there to take care of her."

"So you snuck back in and . . ."

"I got Daisy. She'll be safer in the building."

"If you can figure out where to take her," Liam said.

He looked down at Daisy. She was busy sniffing at the carpet in the hallway. She had no idea that there was no one to take care of her.

"What about Shayla?" Liam asked. There was no way Daisy could fit into the chaos of his home. And now that he knew she came from an infected apartment, he didn't even want to be near her.

Ai hesitated, then she said, "Maybe her dad will let her keep Daisy. Let's go find out."

Ai reached out for Daisy's leash, but Liam shook his head.

"You need to go home and quarantine. I'll handle it."

"But . . ."

"Go home!" Liam said firmly.

"Okay, okay," Ai said with her hands up.

"You take the stairs. I'll take the elevator," Liam said.

"Text me after you leave her," Ai said. Then she turned and went running down the hall.

Liam walked in the opposite direction and stopped at the elevators. He thought about how horrible Mrs. Connor must have felt if she couldn't even get out of bed to feed Daisy. And what about the other older neighbors, like Mr. Ye? The days of the quarantine were so full of his siblings' antics that he didn't think about how hard it must be for other people.

He covered his finger with the hem of his shirt and pushed the button. His mind wandered through the faces of his neighbors. Between fighting off the threat of panic and helping his mom, he felt like he was drowning. But suddenly, he was thinking about the rest of the building. What if everybody was suffering? What if he wasn't the only one having a hard time?

Special Delivery!

The pattern on the fabric looked blurry. Shayla wiped her eyes with the back of her hand and blinked away the tears. Usually, phone conversations with her mother were full of laughter and excitement, but this time her mom had nothing but bad news. Not only did her mom have to cancel her flight to New York, but she had to cancel their entire spring break trip. No beach, no spa, and no hotel pool. Her mom had promised they would make up for it in the summer, but it didn't make Shayla feel any better.

She tried her best to push away her sadness and focus on her work. She was halfway through cutting out the shapes for a stack of masks when the doorbell rang. Her father paused the sewing machine and looked back at her over his shoulder.

"Sassy, get the door," he said.

Shayla slid her fingers out of the scissors. They

were sore, with red marks on her thumb and middle finger. Shaking her hand, she walked over to the door and stood on her tiptoes to look through the peephole, but there was no one out there.

"You sure someone's at the door?" she asked.

"The doorbell rang," her father replied.

She cracked the door open and peeked out. Immediately, she felt something soft nudging her leg.

Looking down, she was surprised to find Daisy sniffing at her feet.

"How'd you get here?" she asked with a grin. She knelt to pet Daisy.

"Who is it?" her father asked, stopping the machine again.

"Ummmm." Shayla opened the door wider. Daisy scampered a few steps into the apartment, then jerked to a stop. Her leash, which was wrapped around the door handle, prevented her from going any farther.

"What's going on here?" her father asked.

"This is Daisy," Shayla said. She tugged the leash until Daisy backed closer to the door.

"Why is there a dog in my home, Shayla Asia Simone?"

She snuck a glance up at her father. His face was full of confusion.

"Someone left her here," she said with a shrug.

Her father took his foot off the pedal of the sewing machine and swiveled his body to face her.

"How do you know the dog's name?"

"It's Mrs. Connor's," she said.

"This is the dog you and your friends decided it was your job to rescue?"

Shayla nodded.

"And what is it doing here?"

"I don't know, Daddy," Shayla said, holding Daisy's leash tightly. "I really don't."

"So let's bring it back," Shayla's dad said, standing up.

"Bring her where?" Shayla asked. "Mrs. Connor is in the hospital."

Shayla's dad walked over to her and gave her one of his *you've-got-to-be-kidding-me* stares.

"Oh, you and your friends must think you're slick."

Shayla let go of Daisy and pressed her hands together.

"Daddy," she said. She made her face as serious and her voice as calm as she could. "I promise you that I don't know how Daisy got here. I didn't plan this with my friends. We left her in Mrs. Connor's apartment."

Shayla's dad stared at her for a long time, as if he could read the truth on her face. As they stood there facing each other, Daisy crept out from behind Shayla and started to nose at her dad's feet. He sighed, then his shoulders finally relaxed.

"Can we keep her?" Shayla asked.

Her dad narrowed his eyes at her and she held her breath waiting for his answer.

●●●

The next morning, when Shayla asked to go to Ben's apartment to get dog food, her father shook his head.

"Do you know what it means to be grounded AND quarantined?" he asked.

Shayla nodded. She knew it meant that she couldn't do anything at all, but she figured she could at least get what she needed to feed Daisy.

Her dad put both hands on her shoulders.

"Until I tell you otherwise, there's only one reason you can leave this apartment—and that's to walk the fur ball," he said.

"Soooooooooo, I can't go pick up her food?" she asked in a low voice, in case the question annoyed him.

"No interacting with people. You don't talk to any-one. You don't touch anyone. You don't look at anyone.

And when you take Daisy for her walks, you keep your head down, you avoid people, you let the dog do its business, and you come right back upstairs."

"For fourteen days?" Shayla asked.

"For at least fourteen days," her father said. "I might decide you need more time to learn your lesson."

"But . . ."

"One more thing," her dad said before she could get her question out. "You better not get me sick while we're locked up in here together either. No kisses and no hugs."

"But Dad, we're already . . ."

Her father held his hand up in the air and backed away from her.

"I don't want any of your little spit and droplets and anything else that comes out of that nose and mouth to spray on me. Is that fair?"

Shayla pouted and swiveled away from her father. She fell back onto the couch and watched Daisy sniffing at the floor.

"Shayla, look at me," her father said. He had that deep tone in his voice that he used when he was serious.

Shayla looked up at him. He didn't blink or offer her one of those big blinding smiles that always made her warm inside. He spoke slowly and firmly.

"You and your friends made a choice and now there are consequences. You didn't protect yourself and now you have to protect me and everyone else. Is that fair?"

Shayla nodded.

"I can't hear you," he said.

"Yes, Daddy," she said with a sigh. "It's fair."

●●●

Shayla's cell phone buzzed. To her surprise, it was a text from Ai.

Ai

 Did you get your special delivery? 🐶 🐶 🎁

Shayla

You left Daisy for me?

Ai

 👣 💨

Shayla's heart leapt. Ai had done something nice for her. Did that mean she'd actually forgiven her?

Shayla

You took her from Mrs. Connor's apartment?

Ai

Shayla broke into a broad grin.

Thief!

Ai

I saved her!

They would have put her in a shelter!

Shayla knelt down and patted her legs. Daisy scampered up to her, resting her tiny paws on Shayla's knees. For a few minutes, Shayla was so filled with joy that she forgot she was grounded. But as soon as her dad got back with the dog food from Ben's apartment, she felt heavy again.

She tried to ignore how tense the air was as she struggled with the can opener. Exactly how did he expect her to stay away from him? Did that mean they couldn't eat dinner together? And they couldn't have dance challenges or play video games?

After three or four tries, she finally pierced the can with the blade of the can opener. As she heard the hiss of air from inside the can, she was drawn into the magic of machines. If you didn't know how to operate them, they were useless—but if you knew what to do with them, they were like magic.

Twisting the handle to cut through the metal top,

Shayla thought friendships were a little like machines. They were useless if they didn't run properly. After so many months of not being friends with Ai, Shayla felt like she just got a little taste of what it felt like when their friendship was working. Without a word, even while they were stuck in two different apartments, Ai had managed to bring fun into Shayla's isolation—and make Daisy's life better too.

The Longest
Week Ever

Being quarantined at home with his parents was the worst punishment Ben could think of. He was trapped. Before quarantine, any time he heard their voices rise, tight and spiky with anger, he could put on his shoes and go to the park, visit friends, even roam the hallways—do anything but listen to their love unraveling.

It felt like the quarantine had shaken something horrible loose in his apartment. It used to feel like his parents were trying to protect him from their disagreements; they used to hide their fights behind closed doors, but now they would start arguments right in front of his face, unleashing harsh words and speaking in cold tones as if he wasn't even in the room.

Ben pressed his hands against his ears, but it didn't block out the sounds.

"You said you would be patient," he heard his father yell. "Do you know what patience means?"

"It doesn't mean you keep me trapped in this city until I die. We've been here for twenty years. I can't take it anymore!"

He heard a thud in the living room and his heart squeezed.

"Are you trying to hurt me?" his father yelled.

"It was an accident," his mother yelled back.

Ben felt his heart pounding really hard. His mind ping-ponged back and forth between the possibility of his dad hurting his mom and his mom hurting his dad. All of a sudden he felt like he had to escape, but how could he get away in his own home? He looked around his room, searching for some way to get farther away from his parents' voices. He opened his closet, but it was crammed with clothes, games, and shoes. He flipped his sheets up and looked under his bed, but it was dark and dusty. He was fantasizing about sneaking out when he had an idea.

The thought of sneaking out made him remember afternoons of building forts and crazy obstacle courses at Shayla's apartment while her father's music blasted in the background. He couldn't go to Shayla's, but maybe he could bring some of her fun to his room.

Excited, he trooped into the kitchen with his head down. If he didn't catch his parents' eyes, he could pretend they weren't there. Blocking out the angry pitch of their voices, he grabbed one of the kitchen chairs and dragged it down the hall to his room. As he went back and forth from his room to the kitchen, he imagined his parents existed in two different universes, separated by miles and miles of silence.

When he collected all the chairs from the dinner table, he shut his door and stared at them. *What can I build?* he asked himself. Shayla was the one with the ideas and he was the one with the plans. He suddenly remembered one of the last things they had talked about building before Shayla had decided hanging out with him wasn't fun anymore. He looked up at the ceiling, down at the chairs, then back up at the ceiling. They had promised to build a super-tall tower. Now Ben had a chance to build something that was taller than anything he had built with Shayla before—and he could do it all alone.

He got busy stacking chairs, starting with a base of two chairs side by side. He flipped a chair upside down, rested it on the backs of the bottom two chairs, and climbed up to keep stacking the chairs one on top of the other until they towered above him.

He needed sheets for the next stage of his project, so he tightened his face and marched out of his room, pretending his parents were a pair of squawking birds. As he yanked open the doors to the linen closet, a few words from their argument fell into his ears. He heard "hate," "never," "waste of my life." Squeezing a pile of sheets between his palms, he rushed back to his room and shut the door behind him.

After he had tied the sheet corners to the top chair, he stood back to admire his work. The sheets cascaded down from his tower and puddled down to the floor. He stretched out the edges and he anchored them with books, then he peeked inside. It was dark and cozy like a cave.

Ben grabbed a few pillows and Bucky and slipped into the tent. He rested Bucky on the floor and settled down on the pillows to enjoy his hideaway. For twenty blissful minutes, he watched Bucky crawl around and read comics using the flashlight on his phone. Then his alarm rang. He rushed to turn it off but he wasn't quick enough. His parents' argument fell silent and he heard footsteps coming down the hall. He placed Bucky back in his tank and jumped into his desk chair. He was just reaching for his laptop when his mother opened the door.

"Are you . . ." She fell silent when she saw his tower.

Ben watched her face in nervous silence. Her eyebrows squeezed up in confusion, then her face softened with sadness. She walked over to his desk and ruffled his hair.

"You made a hideout?" she asked.

Ben could tell she was trying to sound cheerful, but there was no excitement in her voice. She sounded worried.

"Is it . . . ?" She stopped talking and rubbed her temples. Ben watched her close her eyes and rake her fingers through the short hair on the sides of her head. "You can hear us, can't you?" she finally said.

Ben nodded, staring at the stickers on his laptop before sneaking another look at his mother.

"I wish we could soundproof your room," she said, flipping her long bangs out of her eyes with a savage jerk of her head.

"I wish you would stop fighting," he said back.

"Me too," his mom said sadly. For a few seconds, she got very quiet. Then she snapped to attention and checked the fitness tracker on her wrist.

"Don't you have class now? Why aren't you signed on?"

Ben flipped his laptop open. The truth was that he had forgotten about class. Hiding out in his tent, he had forgotten about school and his parents' fighting.

His mom tapped the desk. "Get your notebooks and get signed in to class."

Ben pressed on the power button.

"Are you done..." He glanced past his mom and looked into the hallway.

"Are we done fighting? The fireworks are over. Your dad is taking his work calls in the living room, I'm going to work in the bedroom, and you'll be at your desk. Everyone will be focusing."

When Ben didn't say anything else, his mom clapped her hands.

"Hop to it," she said, moving toward the door. "Class can't start until you sign on."

"Mom?" he asked, stopping her before she could walk away.

When she turned back, Ben finally looked at

her—really looked at her, his eyes pleading for her to tell him the truth.

"You would never hurt Dad, would you?"

His mother gasped a sip of air, like the question had shocked her.

"No, cariño, no," she said, reaching out to squeeze his arm. "I would never!"

"And Dad . . . he wouldn't . . ."

Ben's mom shook her head sharply. "No. He would never."

Then her face melted with sadness. She reached for Ben's hands.

"We're fighting because we disagree, not because we don't love each other. We would never hurt each other and we would never hurt you."

The computer screen blinked on and Ben busied himself searching for the link to his class video. All the while, his mind was spinning. What did his mom mean when she said they would never hurt him? They hurt him every time they fought. And the more horrible their fights were, the more they hurt him.

"Are you on?" his mother asked.

Ben plugged in his headphones and he nodded, pretending to be concentrating on the screen. As soon as his mother left the room, he scooped the laptop and his notebook off the desk and carried them into his tent. He had lied about being signed into class, but he didn't feel bad about it. They were all lying to one another and it seemed like they were all afraid to tell the truth.

It's Lonely Being Alone

Ai lay on her back on the windowsill. There were three other people in her home, but she still felt alone. She stared up at the hanging plants, with their ivy leaves that spilled down toward her. In between the plants was a sculpture of the goddess Dewi Sri flying overhead. Carved from wood, the goddess had a peaceful face and beautiful green-and-yellow wings.

Dewi Sri was her mom's favorite goddess, and in better times, her parents would entertain Ai with dramatic stories about the goddess's life. Dewi Sri's story was full of so many twists and turns that her parents never seemed to run out of new tales. Every time her parents told her a new story, she'd run to get her paper and colored pencils so she could draw the gods and animals Dewi Sri crossed paths with and all the plants she had grown from her body. But now that her parents had stopped telling her stories, she drew the same stories over and over.

Ai climbed down from the windowsill. With nothing better to do, she decided to draw a new picture of Dewi Sri. But this time, she planned to draw her flying away from the apartment, away from the quarantine, to a beautiful green meadow where people could still play together, a place where helping a neighbor didn't mean you had to spend fourteen days alone at home.

She walked down the hallway, trailing her fingers along the walls. When she reached the doorway of the study, she cracked it open and peeked inside. Her father was lying on the couch, one arm flung out and dangling over the floor, and the other folded over his chest. He slept, softly snoring underneath the huge tapestry hanging on the wall above the couch. The colorful embroidery on the tapestry showed the tree of life blossoming with leaves and beautiful flowers. Ai imagined him lying under the branches of the tree of life with her mother while she and Kartika played nearby.

With his arms flung over his head and bent at odd angles, her father looked just like Arjuna—the colorful Javanese rod puppet he loved to tell stories with. She remembered weekends past, when he would grab Arjuna and race her to the kitchen to put on a play for her mother while she cooked. Ai smiled at the thought of the puppet bobbing up and down with its long arms and sharp, pointy elbows.

Her smile fell when he didn't move. Everything around the apartment reminded Ai of life as a family, but her dad hadn't put on a puppet show since quarantine began, and her mother hadn't bothered to leave the bedroom, let alone cook a meal in the kitchen.

Continuing down the hall, Ai hunched her shoulders and wrapped her arms tightly around herself when she walked past her parents' room. She knew if she opened that door, she would be forced to see a lump of blankets instead of her mother's loving eyes and smiling face. She shivered at the image of her parents' bed with no sign of her mother except a streak of her long knotted hair spilling across the pillow. It was better to keep that door closed unless she wanted to see a ghost.

She went into her room to grab a large sheet of paper and her pastel colors, then walked across the hall to knock on her sister's door.

"Kartika?"

"What?" Kartika yelled from inside the room.

Ai turned the knob and pushed the door open slowly. Seeing Kartika sitting on her bed with her laptop in front of her and stacks of paper surrounding her was something of a relief. Kartika's studying was still a wall that kept Ai out, but at least Kartika was awake. Kartika raised her eyebrows at Ai impatiently.

"Can I color in here with you?" Ai asked.

Kartika pushed her glasses up on top of her head.

"After you went renegade? That's not how quarantine works."

Ai looked down at her feet. She was lucky it was Kartika who answered the door when Ben's mom brought her and Shayla home. Kartika promised she wouldn't tell their dad as long as Ai quarantined and she didn't feel sick in fourteen days. Except for sneaking out to get Daisy, Ai had stayed home for a week. But now she was starting to lose it.

"Well . . ."

With that one word from Kartika, Ai looked up hopefully.

"Why don't you open the door and you lie right there," Kartika said, pointing to the floor. "We can work together, but apart."

"Really?" Ai asked.

"Go for it," Kartika said, motioning to the floor.

Ai snuck a glance at her favorite reading spot on the bright green rug at the foot of Kartika's bed, but Kartika didn't notice. She had already gotten back to work. Glasses on and eyes focused on her computer screen, she was busy taking notes. With a sigh, Ai awkwardly sat down on the bare floor and spread her paper in front of her.

She pulled out the blue pastel. With a few swipes of her arm, she drew a bright blue ocean. If she had wings, that's where she would go. She would fly to the beach and drop down on the sand to drink coconut water, eat roasted fish, and jump through the waves. She switched colors and started sketching out mountains above the ocean. The more she moved her hand back and forth, the calmer she felt.

Her mind drifted away from how lonely she felt and started tumbling through memories. Moments with family and friends bloomed in her mind, then disappeared. As she spread color over the paper, thoughts of Mrs. Connor started to nag at her. If she felt alone in her apartment with three other people, what had Mrs. Connor felt like stuck alone in her apartment, sick for who knows how long? How was everyone else in the building getting by? There had to be more people who needed help.

Her family didn't seem to need her, but maybe other people did.

And just like that, she was struck with a new idea. She stood up abruptly.

"Thanks, Kartika," she said as she knelt to quickly pick up her pastels.

Kartika looked up from her laptop, surprised.

"That was quick," she said.

Ai shrugged. "I'm gonna go start on something else in my room."

"You sure?" Kartika asked.

Ai nodded.

"Are you gonna show me what you did?"

Ai looked down at her drawing. Usually, she would hold her family hostage, describing every little detail of her artwork. Then she would grab her phone and make a video call to her grandparents in Indonesia and California to show off her work. There were so many hours of the past week that she would have loved to talk about her art with Kartika, but now she had something new filling her mind.

"You're not going to tell me about it?" Kartika asked.

Ai held up her drawing. She had drawn the swirling ocean with a mix of bright and dark blues. The sandy beach with speckles of peach and brown and yellow. And tall brown mountains with a sharp black outline. But she had left a hole where she had planned to draw the goddess.

"I drew the beach," she said.

"That's beautiful, Ai." Kartika paused and looked closer at the drawing. "But what's that big white hole right there?"

Ai looked down at the paper. That hole was her. Invisible to everyone in her home—and now that she was in quarantine, she sometimes felt like she had disappeared from the whole world.

"I guess I didn't finish it," she said. The need to start her new project made her want to rush out of Kartika's room.

"Well, come back to draw anytime," Kartika said, but Ai was already gone.

●●●

An hour later, Ai broke her promise to Kartika one last time. She put on her mask and snuck out of the apartment with two sheets of paper in her hand. She rushed to the elevator bank and pressed the button. When the doors opened, she stepped in and taped one of the signs to the elevator wall. Holding the elevator doors open, she paused to admire her work. She read over the sign under her breath. In bright hand-drawn letters, it said, DO YOU NEED HELP? Then in black marker it said, TEXT 679-555-0093 FOR HELP WITH GROCERIES, PACKAGES, OR OTHER SMALL CHORES.

She grinned and popped back out into the hallway to wait for the other elevator. Within fifteen minutes, she had hung both signs and was back home. Her boredom had transformed into anticipation as she hunkered down in her bedroom and stared at her phone. *What will happen now?* she wondered. *Who will be the first one in the building to text for help?*

A Different Kind of Danger

When Liam woke up and heard the sound of the news leaking into his room from the living room, he was confused. His mom had banned the news weeks ago. Ever since the day she came home from work and found him stuck at the kitchen sink, red-faced and gasping, she refused to let him watch anything but cartoons and kids' shows.

He rubbed his eyes and got out of bed. He was surprised to find his mother sitting in the living room, staring at the television and crying.

"Ma?"

His mom jumped and dried her cheeks with the back of her hand.

"What's wrong?" he asked, rushing over to her.

Fumbling for the remote, she clicked off the

television, then threw the remote onto the couch. Before the screen went dark, Liam saw the picture of a man with a broad nose and dark skin staring at him from the television. Under the man's face it said, "George Floyd, 8 minutes and 46 seconds."

"They knelt on his neck." She sniffled.

"Who did?" Liam asked.

"The cops," she said with a shaky exhale. "They knelt on his neck until he was dead."

Liam sat next to his mom in silence. He didn't know what to say. His mother wasn't a crier. He had only seen her do it twice in his life. Both times it was when his sisters were tiny crying babies who always needed to eat or be changed or be rocked. Liam knew exactly what to do if he saw her lying limp on the bed or the couch with sore limbs and no energy left to take care of the pair of crying babies. He would stroke her face and tell her to close her eyes. Then he would scoop up Cayla in one arm and Cara in the other and hustle them out of the room so his mom could rest.

But this was a different kind of crying. It was like something was ripping her up inside.

"I didn't want to watch that," she said, shaking her head. "And I don't want you to watch it either."

"The news?" Liam asked, reaching for the remote.

His mom grabbed his hand.

"Promise me you won't watch the news," she said. "They keep showing him . . ." She trailed off and sniffled again. "They show him . . . dying. You don't need to see that."

Liam dropped the remote.

"Why are they showing that?" he asked.

His mother shook her head. "I don't know."

Liam dropped down on the couch and they sat together in silence for a few minutes. Then she took a deep breath and sighed so loudly that Liam felt the couch shake.

She brushed her hand through his hair. "Do you have class soon?"

Liam nodded, but he wasn't thinking about school. He was thinking about death.

"Well, I don't have to go to work until after your last class, so you can take the laptop to my room. I'll stay out here with the kids so you can get some quiet." She gave him a kiss and stood up. "I'll make you some breakfast."

"Do you think people will keep dying?" he asked, looking up at her.

Her hair was flattened on one side where she had

slept, and she had bags under her eyes. The slump of her shoulders could have been from exhaustion or from sadness. As he waited for her answer, he realized he could have been asking about people dying from the virus or from the cops.

"I hope not." She finally sighed. She kissed him again and pushed him toward the hallway. "Go get ready for school."

Liam went to the bathroom to brush his teeth, but he couldn't shake the man's face. He brushed his hair and dressed with the man's eyes clear in his mind, staring right at Liam as if the man had something to say. As he was grabbing his laptop and his notebooks, his phone pinged. It was a text from Ai. There was no message, just an attachment. He tapped it and saw a photo of a flyer. It said DO YOU NEED NEED HELP? across the top.

Liam

What's this?

Within a few seconds his phone rang.

"It's a good idea, right?" Ai said when he answered.

"What's a good idea?" he asked, whispering as he snuck past the twins' room. He could hear them giggling. The quieter he was, the longer it would be before they came out of their room and started racing through the apartment, screeching at the top of their lungs.

"Helping!" Ai said. "Remember when I told you about Mrs. Connor?"

"Yep," Liam said, dodging toys underfoot as he walked into his mother's room.

"Well, there's more old people in the building," Ai said.

"And they need help?" Liam asked, dumping his laptop and notebooks on his mother's bed.

"And they need help," Ai repeated.

"So you made a sign?" Liam asked. Ai was so excited, he could practically hear her bouncing around as she talked.

"I made two. And I hung them up in the elevators. You should help me."

Liam paused as he was leaning over his laptop to sign in for class.

"I should help you with what?"

"Help me help the people in the building."

Liam looked at the laundry basket full of dirty clothes sitting at the foot of his mother's bed, and the three piles of clean clothes stacked next to the pillows. If he was going to help anybody, he needed to help his mother.

"Liam?!" Ai said. "Are you still here?"

"Mmm-hmmm," Liam grunted. "Just trying to sign on for class. You know, for school?"

Ai laughed.

"I know. I'm ready, I just wanted to talk to you first. Don't you think meeting the neighbors and helping would be fun?"

Liam sighed. "Maybe for you, but I have too much to do. It's a disaster around here."

"But you do stuff at home all the time," Ai said. "Don't you want a break?"

Liam snorted. "You call running around the building helping people a break?"

"Yes, because there's no dirty dishes and no screaming twins," Ai shot back.

"Aren't Shayla and Ben helping you? What do you need me for?" Liam asked, glancing at the clock on his laptop. It was eight thirty on the dot.

Ai was silent for a little while. Then she said quietly, "Actually, they're not. I'm only asking you."

"Me?!" Liam said. He didn't know what to say. He had never been the first person invited to anything. A rush of giddiness suddenly took over his body. He knew something that Shayla and Ben didn't.

"Pleeeaaassseee?" Ai said.

Liam grinned. "Okay, but not today. We have too many classes and my mom is working later."

"Let's start tomorrow," Ai said. "At lunchtime."

"Okay, fine. I'm hanging up now though. Ms. Breaux might not care if you're late, but Mr. O hates it," Liam said.

The phone went silent and Liam busied himself, finding the least messy corner of his mom's bedroom so he wouldn't be too embarrassed by what his classmates saw once the school day began.

One Step Forward, Two Steps Back

The day her quarantine ended, Shayla ran into the living room in her pajamas and danced around behind her father's chair.

"I'm free, I'm free, I'm freeeeeeeee," she sang.

Her father didn't move.

"Daddy!" she yelled, tapping him. "I can hug you now, right?"

Her father pulled the earbuds out of his ears and turned to face her. His eyes were red and he wasn't smiling. Shayla felt all her excitement drain out of her body.

He tugged her toward him, wrapped his arms tightly around her, and brushed his hands over her hair.

"What's wrong, Daddy?" she asked quietly. She wasn't used to seeing him so serious.

"They killed somebody again," he said. Right away she knew he was talking about the cops.

"Again?" Shayla's eyes strayed to the wall just past her father's sewing machine. He had made printouts of the two people who had just died, the same way he had every other time the cops had killed someone. She looked at Breonna Taylor's face—she seemed to be smiling at Shayla from the photo. Then she looked at the other person's face. Ahmaud Arbery was smiling too, and wearing a fancy suit like he was going somewhere nice. They looked so full of life in their photos. She had no idea who they were when they were alive, but now that they had been killed, so many people around the world were connected to them.

Each time it happened, each time a Black person was killed like this, by the police—or even a random White man with a gun—for no reason at all, her father dipped into a deep sadness that filled their apartment. She had been through it with him at least six times that she could remember. He would swing from being terrified about what could happen to her to rage that no one seemed to get arrested. He'd say things about how Americans didn't care when Black people were murdered. How his taxes didn't keep him safe. How horrible it was that a whole community was so disposable, so unimportant that when they died, people just shrugged their shoulders and did nothing.

Every single time, he would rage until his anger burned out and he was left with nothing but heartbreak. When Shayla was younger, she would ask questions. But whenever her father tried to explain, he ended up talking about things she couldn't really understand—economics and slavery, free labor and prison. But the more she learned, the less it made sense. How could history make her less human? How could it be true that she could be casually killed and her murder would mean less than the death of one of her friends? If she thought about it too deeply, she thought her brain would break.

When her father ran out of reasons, he could only say that it had always been this way. When he was a child, his parents tried to keep him safe from police brutality; when her grandparents were children, they could get beat up or murdered for trying to do simple things like use a bathroom or eat at a restaurant; and when her great-grandparents were children, it was even more dangerous. They could be hurt just for words or glances.

As she got older, she stopped asking why Americans thought it was okay to kill Black people. The stories piled onto her shoulders, filling her body with the same sadness that weighed her father down. All the words and explanations and excuses boiled down to one thing: Being Black meant she wasn't as safe and she had to learn to live with it. And that was just the way it was.

She leaned her head on her father's shoulder and wrapped her arms around him. Daisy wriggled her way between them and jumped up to put her paws on Shayla's legs.

Her father smiled. It was one of the smallest, saddest smiles she had ever seen on his face.

"Life goes on," he said, nudging her. "Go take care of that dog before it loses its mind."

Shayla gave her dad a kiss and squeezed him one more time, then she stuffed her sadness down into a tiny ball and tucked it away in her mind so she could move on with her day.

●●●

When Shayla got on the elevator, she saw something that chased the cloud of dark thoughts from her mind. There was a sign taped inside the elevator that had Ai's handwriting. Gripping Daisy's leash, she moved closer to the back of the elevator and read the sign. Ai was doing a whole project that she hadn't told Shayla about!

The elevator doors slid open and Daisy surged forward, tugging Shayla away from the sign. After just a few steps, she slammed right into Liam. The three boxes he was carrying flew from his grasp and clattered to the floor.

"Oh no! Sorry, Liam," Shayla said, bending down to help him pick them up.

She stood up just in time to see Ai rounding the corner with a stack of boxes of her own.

"Wait, what are you two doing?" she asked.

"Helping," Liam said.

"Helping who?" Shayla asked, looking around.

"The neighbors," Ai said. A clipboard sat on top of her stack of boxes.

Shayla darted toward Ai and grabbed the clipboard.

"Deliver groceries to 4B; walk the dog for 7C, morning and evening; pick up packages for 8G," she said, reading aloud from the clipboard.

She looked up at Ai. "We just got out of quarantine. How did you do all this already?"

Ai shrugged. "Guess I've been busy," she said. "Can I have my list back?"

Shayla put the clipboard back on top of Ai's boxes and stood there, speechless, as the elevator dinged. Ai and Liam stepped inside.

"See you in class," Ai said as the elevator doors slid closed.

Shayla stood there motionless, even though Daisy was tugging at the leash. What just happened made no sense. She had apologized to Ai and Ai had brought Daisy to Shayla. Ai wouldn't have given her a special delivery if she hadn't forgiven her, would she? Nothing felt right. Ai was helping people in the building without her and she had just strolled past Shayla like nothing had changed.

Learn from it! she heard her father's voice yell in her mind. That was what he always told her whenever things didn't go her way. He didn't like her to get stuck feeling sorry for herself. *That's life*, he would say. *You are always going to hurt somebody, and somebody is always going to hurt you. But if you don't learn to do better when it happens, you're wasting your time.*

"Okay," Shayla said out loud, like she was answering her father's challenge.

Then she straightened her back and gently tugged Daisy's leash. Following Daisy as she scampered toward the exit, Shayla realized she was going to need a new plan. If her apology didn't work and Daisy wasn't a gift, she was going to try again—and she was going to keep trying everything she could think of to show Ai what their friendship was worth.

Helping Is Healing

Ai wasn't sure how much Liam really wanted to help with the building project, but the more he helped, the happier he seemed every time they met up. That afternoon when it was time to walk a rowdy Alaskan husky and an excitable Doberman pinscher, Ai thought for sure Liam would back out.

"There's only two dogs," she said once they had collected the dogs from the owners. "You don't have to come outside if you don't want to."

Liam held up his hands. They were covered with plastic gloves.

"I'm ready for this," he said.

Ai handed Liam one of the leashes and off they went—both of them leaving the building for the first time in weeks. When they got back with the dogs, they were so energized by the fresh air that they decided to knock on one last door before heading back home to do their schoolwork.

Liam was still laughing about how often Ai got tangled up in the leashes as he knocked on the last door. When it swung open, their faces dropped. It was the mean lady from the building—and that's exactly what they called her: Mean Lady. She never said hello if they were in the elevator together, she didn't hold the door for anybody, and wherever she went she kept a big frown on her face.

Ai and Liam backed away from her door as she stood there looking at them.

"Well?" she asked in a voice that was as crabby as the frown on her face.

"We . . . ummm . . ." Liam started talking, and then stopped just as quickly as he began.

Mean Lady put a hand on her hip. "Why you knocking on my door?" she asked.

"We're here to ask if you needed any help," Ai said.

"You knock on my door to see if I need help," Mean Lady repeated.

"Yes," Liam nodded.

"We have a list," Ai said, waving her clipboard in the air. "We can walk dogs and bring your groceries."

"And help with your mail," Liam chimed in.

"No. I don't need help," Mean Lady said, shaking her head. The frown stayed firm on her face.

Without looking at each other, both Ai and Liam took another step back.

"Okay, well, we can come back in a few days to see if you think of something," Ai said.

Quickly turning away from Mean Lady, Liam said "Bye" over his shoulder.

"Wait!" Mean Lady said. She pushed her door open wider. Concentrating on her foot, she nudged a smooth black rock against the door with the toe of her slipper. When the door stayed open, she turned and walked into her apartment. When she was gone, Ai whispered, "What should we do?"

"Well, she's seen us now, so we have to wait," Liam whispered back.

"What if she doesn't come back?" Ai asked.

"Then we'll go," Liam said. "And we'll never come back. Write down her apartment number."

Just as Ai was telling Liam she'd never forget Mean Lady's apartment number, the lady appeared in the doorway holding out a purple flyer. Ai and Liam looked at each other, then looked back at Mean Lady. She shook the flyer. Liam stepped forward and took it so that both he and Ai could read it. The flyer had a big pair of hands praying on top. It said ONLINE CHURCH underneath the hands.

Ai looked down at the flyer, then up at Mean Lady, down at the flyer, and up at Mean Lady again.

"So . . ."

"How do I do?" Mean Lady asked.

"How do you . . . ?" Ai trailed off as she read the flyer frantically. There was a link for a video meeting with a day and a time.

"I want to do church," Mean Lady said.

"Well, you go on your computer and type this in," Ai said. She pointed to the link on the flyer.

"I try," Mean Lady said, and crossed her arms.

"You have to type exactly what's on the paper," Liam said.

"You come. You show me," Mean Lady said, and turned to walk into her apartment.

Ai took a step toward the door, but Liam blocked her with his hand.

"No," he whispered. "It's not safe. Plus, look how much trouble Shayla and Ben got in. Didn't you learn anything?"

"Ummm, can you bring your computer out here?" Ai yelled down the hall.

Mean Lady grunted, then there was silence.

"Do you think she's coming back?" Liam asked.

Ai shrugged. Her mind slipped to her family and she realized she hadn't thought about them for hours. She hadn't worried about her mother getting out of bed, or her father coming home from work sick. She had been so focused on helping that she had forgotten to be sad. Her eyes popped open a little wider when she realized how much helping the neighbors distracted her. She snuck a glance at Liam. Was it like this for him? She knew a song or a hug or a conversation could help yank him out of a panic attack, so was it possible that helping others gave his mind something else to focus on too?

Before she could ask him about it, she heard the sound of wheels. She peeked down the hallway and saw Mean Lady slowly moving toward them. She was pushing a rickety orange cart with a huge clunky laptop on top of it. Mean Lady pointed to the computer.

"Show me how."

Liam grabbed the flyer from Ai. "Well, it's not today."

Mean Lady pointed again. "Show me."

Ai spun the cart to face her, typed, and clicked,

searching for the Wi-Fi. Then she pushed the cart to Liam.

"It's not connected to Wi-Fi," she said.

Liam found an open network, connected Mean Lady's computer, and pushed the cart back to Ai. She typed in the URL, then spun the cart back around to Mean Lady.

"Okay, you see where it says, 'You are the first person in this meeting'?"

Mean Lady nodded.

"On Sunday, at the time it starts, people will start joining and you will be able to attend church."

"But before that you won't see anything on the screen," Liam chimed in.

"If you don't turn off your computer, you can just keep this screen up, okay?" Ai said.

Mean Lady nodded. Then she looked at both Ai and Liam and said, "Thank you."

Her eyes were wet, like she was going to cry.

Just then the super came by.

"Afternoon, Mrs. Romulus. Are these two bothering you?" he joked.

"No," Mean Lady said with a very serious expression on her face. "They are helping."

"We are helping everybody," Liam said proudly.

"See," Ai said, and handed him her clipboard.

The super was quiet for a few minutes, grunting as he read.

"I'm impressed. How do I get on the list?"

"You have to ask me," Ai said. She crossed her arms and tried to look important.

"Well . . ." The super paused and waved to Mrs. Romulus as she shut her door. "Tomorrow morning, ten o'clock, the lobby. I need all four of you."

"Ummmm," Ai said. She looked uncertain.

"Oh, I thought all I had to do was ask you," the super said.

"Well . . ." Ai said, and fell silent. They were one day out of quarantine, so there was no way she was going to have Shayla's and Ben's parents think she was asking them to help. Plus, if she asked Shayla to help, she was sure Shayla would think Ai had forgiven her. She wanted to, but it wasn't that easy to take a friend back after they'd abandoned you. Especially when they were all stuck in the building together and there was no way for Shayla to prove that she really wanted to be friends.

"What's the problem?" the super asked. "You think I don't need help? I'm your neighbor too!"

"Liam and I can help but I'm not sure about Shayla and Ben. It's just that . . ." Ai trailed off.

"It's just that their parents want them to be safe," Liam said, jumping in. "If you ask, you can tell them that you have everything they need to stay safe."

Ai nodded in agreement.

The super looked down at them, his dark eyes darting back and forth between Ai's face and Liam's as if trying to figure out what they weren't telling him.

"Okay, fine," he said. "Meet me on the sixth floor at nine tomorrow and we'll ask them together. Deal?"

"Deal," Ai and Liam answered together.

●●●

As Ai headed home, she couldn't help but think about how Liam was going back to a lively home full of activity and she was headed to an empty one. She lived with the exact same number of people as Liam, but sometimes it felt like no one lived there at all. She'd had more conversations offering to help the neighbors than she'd had during the whole two weeks quarantined at home. She replayed all the smiles and thank-yous that she had received through-out the day. She was exhausted, but she was zinging with excitement. Helping the neighbors had changed the way she felt. She wasn't invisible after all. Even if her family had lost the ability to show up for one another, she could show up for her neighbors. She had the power to make people's hard times a little easier.

19

A Welcome Distraction

On the first Saturday after the quarantine, Ben dressed quickly. He dropped some food in Bucky's tank, grabbed his skateboard, and sped out of his room. As he rushed through the hallway, he thought about how great it would feel to go outside again.

He yanked the door open and took a step backward. "Ummm, hello?"

The super, Ai, Shayla, and Liam were standing there.

"Are your parents home?" the super asked.

Ben nodded. He raised his eyebrows at his friends as if asking them a question, but they just shrugged and looked back at him with mysterious smiles.

●●●

Agreeing to help meant leaving his skateboard at home. The super insisted on them taking separate elevator trips to get down to the lobby, then he led them through the service door into a dimly lit hallway. It was gray with marked-up walls and a concrete floor.

"I dragged you all down here to see if you would expand your helping mission to join my antivirus team."

"Our helping what?" Ben asked.

"Oh," Shayla said. "Didn't you know? Ai and Liam have a little helpers club."

Ai narrowed her eyes at Shayla.

"Is someone feeling left out?" she asked, crossing her arms.

Shayla rolled her eyes.

Ben sighed. With Shayla on his left and Ai on his right, he felt like he was back in the middle of another battle.

"So, I'm on my own here," the super said, trying to refocus the conversation. "With the staff staying home, I'm doing the work of three. Everyone saves their recycling for the weekends. So collecting it from all the floors and prepping it for pickup is pretty much an all-day job, which means it's really hard to disinfect the building on weekends." He held up a spray bottle and waved it in the air.

"So you want us to . . ." Liam said.

"Disinfect!" the super said. "If you're still in the helping spirit."

"We are!" Ai chimed in.

"Good! So here's what I need: cleaning and wiping down the elevator buttons and the outside of the elevator doors."

"On every floor?" Shayla asked.

"Every floor," the super said. "Can you imagine how many people touch the surfaces every day?"

"What about the trash room?" Liam asked.

"That would be great," the super said. "The door handle, the faucets on the sink, and the handle to the trash chute."

"Ewwww," Shayla said. "The trash room stinks."

"Shhh," Ben said.

The super laughed. "I didn't mentioned the trash room because I didn't want to scare you on your first day," he said. "But I'm a one-man band, and I can use all the help I can get."

Ben squinted as he calculated how long it would take to wipe down the elevators. It would take some time, but not enough to give him the day of freedom he imagined.

"We'll do the trash rooms," Ben said. The extra

work would give him a good long break from his parents.

"On all the floors?" Shayla asked again, her eyes bugging out.

"People live on all the floors." The super laughed.

"Is it too much work for you?" Ai asked in a mocking tone. "I would have thought you would have loads of free time now that you're not running after Megan and Gemma anymore."

Ben heard Shayla gasp.

"Let's just keep it together," he said. He understood why Ai was upset, but he was done with everyone spreading their grouchiness everywhere. Of course it hurt to watch a friend avoid you, but Shayla was back now. He had forgiven her and he thought it was time for Ai to forgive her too.

He turned back to the super, his mind working to push away Shayla's and Ai's bickering. He tried to imagine the logistics of the super's work. There were fifteen floors in the building. How could one person take care of everything?

"Are you saying you do this every day?"

The super shrugged. "I split up the big jobs so I can make time for disinfecting. I've got to take care of the carpet on all the floors, the roof, the community room, the bike room, the laundry room, the lobby; it all has to get cleaned. Then there's the trash and the recycling, and helping residents when things break . . ." The super let out a big breath. "And now the virus. I try to wipe down the elevators and the building entrance three times a day."

"Three times a day!" Ben tilted his head and stared at the ceiling as he made a few quick calculations. "That's twenty-one cleanings a week; eighty-four cleanings a month!"

Ben looked around. He was happy to see Shayla and Ai had finally stopped glaring at each other. Everyone was staring at the super in shock. They had no idea he was doing so much work.

"The virus can live on metal surfaces for three days. The less time it sits on one of our surfaces, the less likely it is to get someone sick."

"So if we help you, we're, like, saving everybody from getting sick," Liam said.

"That's the plan," the super said with a deep sigh. Then he fell quiet. For a few seconds, his usual cheerful, friendly expression disappeared. Ben saw nothing but exhaustion and even a little bit of fear on his face.

"Well, we're part of the plan now," Ben said. He had

no idea what this helping club was that Ai and Liam were doing, but now he had an important mission— and it seemed like a much better distraction than escaping with his skateboard or making a fort out of chairs.

Reunited

"See," Shayla said. "This is Ai's and Liam's helpers club." She pointed to Ai's sign.

The four of them had wrestled on plastic gloves and stood at opposite corners of the elevator clutching their cleaning supplies.

Ben turned and read the sign and Liam blushed, embarrassed that he was dragged into Ai's and Shayla's feud.

"We're all in the club now." Ben shrugged.

As the elevator slid past the sixth floor, Liam pushed away his embarrassment by imagining what was happening in his apartment. He thought of his mother sitting at the kitchen table paying the bills while Cayla and Cara swirled around her like hyperactive, noisy sharks. Caught between his mother's exhaustion and the Quartet's conflicts, Liam had a tight, spiky feeling tugging at his chest. When the elevator reached the top floor, he decided it had been too long since all four of them were together. He wasn't going to waste it worrying about things he couldn't control.

When they trooped off the elevator, Liam whirled around and held his hands up like he had an emergency statement.

"I received a top secret message from headquarters," he said.

For a few seconds, they all looked confused.

"First Officer Christopher," Liam said to Ben. "Do you have the X-ray glasses?"

Liam could see Ben's eyes light up with excitement as he lifted his hand to his glasses.

"X-ray glasses activated!" he said.

"X-ray glasses on," Liam commanded.

They all mimed putting on X-ray eyeglasses. Liam held up his hand and pretended to read a message from it.

"The aliens have invaded. Height: Smaller than one inch. Powers: Can eat through concrete and metal. Weapon: Special alien-melting potion. Mission: Clear bunker of aliens. End of message. Message self-destruct set for five, four, three, two, one."

"Boom," they all said together, mimicking the sound

of the message exploding. Just like old times.

"Trash chute and sink in my sights," Ai said.

"Attack set for stairwell," Shayla said.

"Elevator doors and buttons?" Liam said to Ben.

Ben gave Liam a salute. Then the friends threw themselves into the work, entertaining one another with what they thought squealing aliens would sound like. When they were finished, Liam pretended to talk into his wristwatch.

"Aliens neutralized on top floor. I repeat, aliens neutralized on top floor," he said.

Shayla hit the button for the elevator.

"Only thirteen more floors to go," she said.

By the time they hit the eighth floor, Liam had created a complex series of alien cries that they all followed. He would start, then Ben would echo him. Ai would follow with a high-pitched shriek, and Shayla rounded it out with a low groan. Even though they had done it over and over, they could barely get through the sounds without breaking down into laughter.

On the seventh floor, Liam created a game that involved jumping over a row of spray bottles and tossing and catching the cleaning cloths. When Ben tried to copy Liam, he tripped and tumbled against the wall with a loud thud. Ai and Shayla burst out in uncontrollable laughter and one of the apartment doors swung open.

"What is happening out here?" A man stood in the doorway of the apartment and glared at the friends.

"Oh, sorry, Mr. Carl," Liam said. "We're just helping the super with cleaning."

"Well, this is entirely too much noise for cleaning," he complained. "I am trying to work in here!"

"Oh, we'll be more quiet," Ben said.

"I hope so," Mr. Carl said, and slammed his door shut.

The second the door was closed, they all burst out in soft giggles. With fake serious faces, they quit the dead alien cries. As soon as they got to the next floor, the fun started back up again as they completed their duties.

Before Liam knew it, they were on the second floor, wrapping up the last of the cleaning. He was sweaty and his arms hurt, but the soreness was balanced by all the laughter that still seemed to be bouncing around inside him.

At Liam's command, they ran through their alien cries one last time. Shayla was just finishing the final sound when another apartment door opened. This time instead of an angry neighbor in the doorway, Mrs. Lakshmi was there with a small child clinging to her legs and a baby strapped to her chest.

"Paz just wanted to see what you all were doing," she said with a smile.

Paz jerked forward, trying to run out of the apartment, but Mrs. Lakshmi was faster than him. She grabbed him by the shoulder and pulled him back toward her. Kneeling, she put her face close to his.

"I said I would open the door if you did what, Paz?"

The little boy didn't answer; he just looked down at his feet.

"Okay," she said. "If you don't remember, we'll just go back inside."

"No, no, no," Paz yelled. "If I stay inside."

"Inside," Mrs. Lakshmi repeated to him firmly.

Paz pouted and leaned against the doorframe. Ai sat on the carpet and explained what she was doing, showing him the disinfectant and the cloths. Ben and Shayla split up to finish their jobs.

"Thank you," Mrs. Lakshmi said, looking at Liam and Ai. "First you deliver my diapers and now you're cleaning? It's amazing what you are doing to help. You're great kids!"

Liam smiled at Mrs. Lakshmi, but he felt like he couldn't move. The compliment made him feel warm inside, but the exhausted expression on her face reminded him of his mother. He started to feel heavy, like all the fun had leaked out of his body. While he was having fun, what were Cara and Cayla up to? Were they upstairs driving his mom crazy or were they having a calm day? He stood there feeling stuck as guilt snaked through his body then settled in the pit of his stomach like a heavy stone.

●●●

When Liam got home, the apartment was quiet. Toys were scattered all over the floor and a pair of princess dresses were hanging over the arm of the couch. His mom was standing in front of the window all alone.

"Mom," he said, rushing toward her, but she held a hand up to stop him.

"No, no, no," she said firmly. "Take off your shoes, go wash your hands, and change your clothes."

Liam couldn't believe that for a few seconds he had forgotten about the virus. He rushed to his room and threw his mask and gloves into the trash. In the bathroom, he rubbed the soap into his hands and rinsed them. After changing into a clean set of clothes, he headed back to the living room. On his way, he saw that his sisters were playing quietly in their room.

By the time he made it back to his mom, that heavy feeling in his stomach started to disappear. He put his hands on her shoulder and kissed her on the cheek.

"We killed so many germs today!"

"Did it make you feel better?" She turned and rubbed his back.

He nodded. He had spent so much time thinking about the invisible viruses around him—how they could attach to his clothes, his hair, his own skin, and make him sick—that he hadn't thought that there was invisible protection too. Even though there was lots of danger out there, there were forces of good too, like the super doing things Liam didn't even know about to help keep everyone safe.

"Did you know the super wipes down everything three times a day?"

"I didn't know that, honey," she said with a big smile.

She didn't look exhausted.

"So how was today?" he asked. "Were the girls . . ."

"They were the same as always," his mom said.

"Today, it was all about who is the tallest between them and all the crazy things they could do to get taller. Did you see their potion in the bathroom?"

Liam smiled and rested his head on his mom's shoulder. He had felt so good being out with his friends, but he felt good coming back home too. It wasn't easy taking care of his siblings, but he did it because he needed to know that everything was okay at home.

"I'm going to make dinner," his mom said.

"I'll help."

"No," his mom said, playfully pushing him toward the sofa. "You need to take a break after all that cleaning."

Liam sank down into the couch. He felt full of warmth.

"I'm so proud of you," his mom said from the kitchen.

Liam burst into a big grin. It felt good to realize that he had more power than he thought. He could help his mother at home, and he could help the super push away the virus. His mom and friends did so much to help him deal with his panic, and it felt good to know there was something he could do to help keep everyone safe.

Music Makes a Powerful Sound

Shayla squinted at the computer screen. Her eyes darted from left to right while she read the project Ms. Breaux was showing on the screen.

Country Study

Research an African animal and its ecosystem. Your project must include a poster illustrating the animal at different stages in its life cycle and a three-page report about its defining features, its adaptations, and its role in the local ecosystem.

Shayla looked up at the world map on the wall above the computer. It was totally different from the ones at school. All the maps at school made North America and Europe look so much bigger than they really were. At home, the map showed that Africa, Asia, and South America were the biggest landmasses on the globe.

"Africa is a continent, not a country," she muttered, then she clicked the icon to raise her hand.

"Yes, Shayla?"

"When we studied the country of China, we had to do reports on the people and the culture. Can we do reports on people from the continent of Africa?"

Shayla heard her father stop his sewing behind her. She unplugged her headphones and leaned to the side so he could see the screen. Ms. Breaux was quiet for so long that Shayla clicked the volume to make sure the sound was working.

"The Africa unit," Ms. Breaux finally said, "is connected to our study of animals and ecosystems. Of course people are an important part of ecosystems, so if you would like to include people in your ecosystem, you are free to do so, but you will only be graded on the animal and ecosystem research."

Shayla heard her father's sewing machine start again. She plugged her headphones back in and leaned her head in her hand. Her eyes drifted to the picture book of African queens and kings propped up on the top of the bookshelf to her left. She didn't think those queens and kings would want her to go along with school projects that pretended their history didn't exist. When class was over, Shayla swiveled around and stared at her father's back.

"You okay, Daddy?" she asked.

His machine paused again. He turned to face her.

"You're the one getting half an education. Are you okay?"

Right above her father's sewing machine was a framed poster of the Black Panther Party's Ten-Point Program. It was all about food, education, housing, and safety. Things her father said Black people still didn't have today. Looking around the living room, she was struck by how nothing reflected on the walls of her home was reflected in the things she learned in school. Along with the world map and the Black Panther poster, there was a poster of Black inventors they never learned about in social studies and a poster of massacres of Black communities that they never learned about in history.

Her father always said he was in a battle for her brain. He said if he left it up to the school system, all she would know about Blackness was slavery and civil rights. What she learned—or didn't learn—in school about Blackness could make her hate herself, and make her classmates think there was nothing important about Black people.

"I'm going to write about people in my report," Shayla said.

Her father gasped. "You're going to do extra work?"

She pointed to the bottom shelf of the bookcase.

"I'm your daughter. My whole life is extra work," she said.

The bottom shelf was crammed with colored paper–covered reports her father made her write on the weekends about the history of Black people around the world. Anything could trigger a report—unfairness at her school, a troubling story on the news, an interesting conversation with a friend.

Her father tapped his temple. "Now you're getting it. You're a Black girl in America. You're always going to have extra work."

Shayla's phone chimed. She picked it up and saw a message from Ai.

Ai

I'm writing about people too.

Shayla sighed and dropped her hands in her lap. That's the kind of friend Ai was. Half the reports Shayla had written about Black people, Ai had written too.

It doesn't mean anything, Shayla told herself firmly.

Ai would always do the right thing, whether she was friends with Shayla or not—and Shayla knew she had more work to do if she ever wanted to be true friends with Ai again.

●●●

Delivering mail wasn't Shayla's idea of a good time, but she was determined to prove to Ai that she was trustworthy. So when the Quartet met up to deliver mail to the neighbors, she decided to keep her mouth shut and work hard. When they got to the last of the packages—a huge box that was taller than all of them—they decided to work together to deliver it.

Shayla stayed focused and kept silent so she wouldn't annoy Ai. She grabbed the dolly from the hallway and helped as everyone else wrestled the box onto it. In the elevator, they cracked one another up, guessing what could be in the box. Was it a refrigerator? A super-big box of adult diapers? A unicorn? No one was sure what was in it, but coming up with guesses was the most fun Shayla had all day.

When they rolled the dolly to the apartment and rang the doorbell, they heard the sound of wild jazz blasting. It wasn't the type of tinkly jazz that usually played in elevators. It was the kind of chaotic and noisy sounds Shayla's dad liked to play while he was working. With that kind of jazz, Shayla never knew what she would hear. The horn might blare like a freight train or squeal like a cat. The drums might sound like a herd of cattle trampling on the floor, or like the tinkling of glass smashing against the concrete. Since George Floyd's death, it was the only kind of jazz he played as he sat hunched over the sewing machine, disappearing inside the chaos of sound.

A man with a huge shock of white hair and dark wrinkled skin opened the door. He had a mask with music notes on it and a twinkle in his eye.

"Hi, Mr. Grove," Shayla said.

"Sassafras!" Mr. Grove said. "You're an angel for bringing me my cello."

"A cello!" Ai said. They all started laughing—their guesses were way off!

"Sassafras?" Ben said.

"Yep," Mr. Grove said. "She's as tall as a sassafras tree. Now what are we going to do about this box?" he asked, scratching his head.

"It's not that heavy," Shayla said.

"We can take it off the cart and push it into your apartment," Liam said.

"Let's do it," Mr. Grove said. "And then y'all can help me with one more thing."

Mr. Grove opened his door wide and stood aside while they pushed the box into the hall.

"That's good, that's good. Now get on out of here," he said as soon as they pushed the box past the open door. "I don't want nobody's parent telling me I put they kids in danger. Scat."

When they were back outside the apartment, Mr. Grove said, "I'll be right back."

When he returned, he had a saxophone hanging around his neck and a box of instruments in his hands.

"Wow, Mr. Grove, you play the saxophone AND the cello?" Ben asked.

"I play the sax, don't know much about the cello. But that's how you keep the brain cells young—always keep learning. Now . . ." Mr. Grove put a box down on his welcome mat. "Grab an instrument."

Then he lifted his saxophone and said, "Follow my lead."

Mr. Grove started blowing a wild, fast tune on his horn. After a minute or so, he pointed the horn at

Liam. Liam lifted a mallet and started hitting the shiny metal triangle he was holding. He pointed to Ai next. She tapped out a beat on the tambourine she was holding. Mr. Grove cued Ben to join in and he started hopping up and down, shaking a big gourd that was covered with beads. Finally, Shayla got her turn to jump in with the xylophone. She tried to play with the heart as Mr. Grove always told her to—even when she was just learning a song.

But before long, Shayla felt like the music was carrying them along. She could hear Liam's tinkling, Ben rattling the gourd, and Ai shaking the tambourine. It felt like they were talking to one another, learning how to make their sounds link up and fly through the air together.

As Shayla focused on the music, her mind went swirling through memory. Some of the sounds made her think about how hard she tried to be friends with Megan. Other sounds made her feel the pain she imagined Ai must have felt when Shayla started avoiding her in school. As the rhythm sped up, she felt the force of Ai's anger, then her own heartbreak.

Mr. Grove stopped playing suddenly and the harmony disappeared. Shayla could hear everyone's instruments clattering and clashing. At the same time, she felt the deep sadness that her mistakes left behind.

"Right on!" Mr. Grove laughed.

"But we were horrible," Ai said.

"You were perfect," Mr. Grove said. "I know where I'm going with this song now. You helped me figure out how the tones sound together. It's like people. Some people mix great. And other people just clash."

Shayla nodded sadly. It was like everything she had heard Ai say dropped from her mind into her heart. She had apologized to Ai, but it was all words and no feeling. She had fought so hard for Megan and Gemma to accept her that she wasn't paying attention to the sounds in her own body. Being with them felt nothing like her friendship with Ai—when they were together, they just made the right sounds. She knew why Ai didn't accept her apology. She was focused on the wrong thing. She was trying to force Ai to understand her—instead of showing Ai that she knew what was most important. She finally understood that Ai wasn't just angry that Shayla was leaving her behind; she was upset that Shayla was throwing herself away by trying to be something she wasn't—to force herself to make sounds that didn't match her true self.

Unrest Everywhere

Right after class ended, Ai checked her clipboard. There was only one task left on the list: dog walking. Liam had helped with the early shift, making an early run to the grocery store and morning dog walking. She and Ben had delivered packages during their lunch break. Shayla was the only one she hadn't called to help that day.

She picked up her phone to text Shayla, but she put it back down without typing anything. She busied herself by putting on a pair of jeans and socks, then dropped the phone into her bag and slung the strap across her body. The second she stepped out of her room, Kartika's door swung open.

"Going somewhere?" Kartika asked.

"Why? Are you spying on me?" Ai asked with her hands on her hips.

Kartika waved her fingers in the air.

"Paranoid," she sang. "I'm just checking on you."

"Oh," Ai said, relaxing. "I'm going dog walking."

"With whose dogs?" Kartika asked, leaning on the doorframe.

"The neighbors'," Ai said.

Kartika looked confused. "Like a job?"

"Like a good neighbor. You know, to help old people stuck in the building."

"Don't tell me you dragged your friends into this?" Kartika asked with an amused grin.

Ai felt a flash of anger she didn't understand. She crossed her arms.

"It's better than being stuck here, all..." She fell silent.

A sad look flashed across Kartika's face. "Go ahead. Finish," she said, moving closer to Ai.

"It's better than being stuck here all alone." Ai felt a rush of emotion sweep through her, so she stiffened her jaw. She didn't want to cry.

Kartika brushed Ai's bangs out of her eyes, then cupped her cheek.

"I know it's hard with Mama—" she said.

"Not just Mama." Ai cut her off. "Ayah . . . You!" It wasn't just her mother. Even her father and Kartika, everyone had disappeared in one way or another. "It's like living in a house with ghosts."

Kartika fell silent. Ai waited for Kartika to get mad, but she didn't. She reached for Ai's shoulders and held her at arm's length. She leaned forward.

"I know this whole thing sucks," she said, locking eyes with Ai. "It's the worst time for me to be busy with school. I don't blame you for feeling abandoned. I can't replace Mama and Ayah, but my door is open. Come talk to me about anything, anytime."

Ai eyed Kartika suspiciously. Her words didn't match her behavior.

"Even when your door is closed?" Ai asked.

"Yeah, as long as you don't have cooties, you can come in."

Ai leaned into Kartika and hugged her tightly. She felt like so much weight was slipping off her shoulders.

"We're going to make it through this together, okay?" Kartika whispered as she hugged Ai back.

Ai nodded. Then she pulled away.

"I have to go. I have six dogs to walk."

"Six? By yourself? You're a saint."

The compliment hit Ai in the chest. With the warmth of Kartika's admiration zinging through her, she pulled her phone out.

Lobby now? 🐶 🐶 🐶 🐶

She sent the text to Shayla before she lost her nerve.

●●●

As soon as Ai and Shayla picked up the dogs, the work of figuring out which were friendly and which should be separated kept them too busy to be awkward with each other. Once the walk was under way, there were six leashes to keep untangled. There was poop to pick up and people to avoid. They walked the dogs three blocks to the park and made the loop around it. By the time they were on their way home, they had figured out how to keep the dogs under control.

Halfway back to the building, they began to hear the sound of people yelling.

"What's that?" Ai asked.

They both went silent as they moved toward the noise.

The sounds of chanting rang out: "George Floyd! Say his name! George Floyd! Say his name!"

"It's a protest," Shayla said. "Like on the news."

Ai felt panicked, like she felt when she forgot about a test or wasn't ready with an answer when Ms. Breaux called on her. Her dad was the one who used to watch the news. Ai learned everything about the world through him. Now that he stumbled home just to sleep, eat, and shower, the news was just another thing Ai was missing out on.

"Did the police kill someone else?" Ai asked.

The chants of the protesters broke into their conversation again. "No justice. No peace. No racist. Police."

"Yep." Shayla nodded.

"A Black man?" Ai asked.

Shayla nodded again. Ai felt like her chest was caving in. Shayla said something but Ai couldn't hear her. Now that they were at the corner, the roar of the protesters drowned out their voices.

"Are you scared?" she asked, but Shayla tapped her ear and mouthed, "I can't hear you."

The dogs started barking and yipping at the river of people streaming onto the sidewalks and filtering down the middle of the street. Ai and Shayla tightened their grips on the leashes as they looked at the crowd of protesters carrying signs with slogans and photos of other Black people who were killed by the police. Ai and Shayla looked at each other and back at the crowd. After a few minutes, Ai tugged on Shayla's arm and pointed away from the noise. Shayla nodded and followed Ai halfway down the block.

"I was wrong," Shayla blurted out as they leaned on a fence, six feet apart, to wait out the protest.

Shayla's expression shook Ai; her eyes were serious and her face was determined. Ai had waited so long for a real apology, but she hadn't imagined it happening like this, with the protest blaring from the corner and the dogs nosing around her feet.

"No, Shayla," Ai said. "We can do this later."

Shayla shook her head forcefully. "No, I have to do it now. How I was acting was really unfair. It was . . ."

Ai watched Shayla searching for the words.

"It was mean," Shayla said. "I don't even know why I was acting that way. You didn't do anything to me."

Ai pulled herself off the fence and nudged away the dogs that were sniffing around her ankles.

"Are you sure we should talk about this now?" she asked. "What about the man who died?"

"Don't you see?" Shayla said. "Anything could happen at any time. I don't want to waste any more time fighting with you."

Ai felt torn. She had so many things she wanted to say, so many words and questions pushing to come out, but a man had died—and whatever had happened to him had to be horrible because there was a protest.

It didn't feel like Ai was the person Shayla should be worried about right now.

"Are you sure?" Ai asked again.

"Yes," Shayla said, holding Ai's gaze. "I'm really sorry."

"Then why did you do it?" Ai asked. "You said nothing happened, but you treated me like crap. How could you be so . . ." Ai's face tightened as all the hurt balled up in her throat. ". . . so fake?" she finally said.

Shayla looked down at her feet and then looked up at Ai.

"I thought I had to change," she said. Her voice was soft, but loud enough for Ai to hear.

"Why?" Ai asked.

"I thought things would be better if I was different." Shayla's voice was still soft, but her words just made Ai feel angrier and angrier.

"Better for who?" Ai's voice was strong with frustration.

"Better for me." Shayla shrugged. Her face was crumpled with pain.

"You weren't happy with yourself? Or you weren't happy with me?" Ai asked.

"I'm just weird," Shayla said. "I'm not girly and I'm not a tomboy. I hate school but I love learning.

Sometimes I don't know what to do with myself. So I thought I could change things if I fit in."

Ai thought she saw tears starting to form in Shayla's eyes, but they didn't spill over.

"Do you forgive me?"

The expression on Shayla's face made Ai's heart hurt. She crossed her arms—which was hard to do with all the leashes.

"Do you still think you have to change?"

Shayla didn't answer, but Ai saw a shift in her eyes. They were glittering, but this time, they weren't glittering with tears; they were shining with determination. For a few seconds, the girls stood there just like that, looking into each other's eyes while the loud yells of the protesters rang out in their ears.

"No justice."

"No peace."

Problems Pile Up

As soon as his first class of the day was done, Ben grabbed his phone. His parents' fighting had reached a new phase. The raised voices and slamming furniture had disappeared. Instead the apartment was dead silent. They filled every room they entered with a cold hostility that felt creepier than the yelling.

Ben

Recycling day! Who can go now?

Then he pressed send and stared intensely at the phone, waiting for a reply. After so much yelling, the arguments had just stopped, but their silence was like a ferocious itch spreading across his skin. Ben's stomach hurt with the anticipation of the explosion that had to be building. He was sure their next outburst would be louder and harsher than any of their other fights. And he didn't want to be around when it happened.

His phone buzzed.

Shayla

Can't. 🍸🍴

Liam

🏠 Have to babysit.

Ben tapped the edge of his desk with his finger and kicked at the rug under his chair as he waited for Ai's response. Finally, his phone buzzed one last time.

Ai

Meet in the lobby?

Ben

K.

●●●

In the lobby, Ben rolled the dolly back and forth as he waited for Ai. It wasn't until the elevator doors opened and he saw Ai standing there that Ben realized what he had done. The four of them were fine together, but when Ben and Ai were alone, it felt more like a competition than a friendship.

He rolled the dolly onto the elevator and Ai punched 12. As the doors slid closed, Ben saw his sign taped on the elevator wall next to Ai's. He flushed with embarrassment. She was so much better at making signs than he was. Her sign was colorful, with blocky letters and different sized words, but his had skinny black letters that were all the same size. It said RECYCLING PICKUP! LEAVE BIG BOXES AND OTHER LARGE RECYCLING ITEMS OUTSIDE YOUR DOOR AT NOON ON WEDNESDAY.

He blurted the first thing that popped into his mind to fill the awkward silence.

"What did you get on the math test?"

Ai sighed. Ben heard a whole ton of annoyance dripping from that one sound.

"Why do you care?"

Ben shrugged. If he had gotten a higher score than her, it would make him feel better about his plain sign.

He always got this way with Ai, but he didn't know why. Ever since she was the top student in second grade, he had kept a secret chart tracking their grades. Ai hated talking about her grades, and she didn't like it when he tried to sneak glimpses of her tests and projects to get data for his chart.

Ben was relieved when the elevator reached the fifteenth floor. They worked together silently to break down the boxes people left outside their apartments, peeling off the tape and folding the boxes flat so they could be stacked on the dolly.

After a few floors, Ben started pouting. They talked only when they needed to coordinate their motions. This wasn't what he left home for. If Liam or Shayla were there, they would be joking around or playing spy games; instead he had annoyed Ai and now they were stuck in this prickly silence.

On the ninth floor, Ben suggested they finish up and go home for lunch. Neither of them sounded excited as they agreed to meet back up after their last class to do the rest of the floors. Their awkwardness turned into curiosity when they saw something strange at the end of the hall.

"Is that . . . ?" Ai asked. She went silent as they both tried to figure out what was waiting for them down the hall.

"I think it's some kind of furniture," Ben said.

"A desk?" Ai asked. "With a mirror?"

"And a broken leg," Ben said as they got closer.

When they reached it, Ben and Ai stood on either side of the furniture, staring down at it. It looked like it belonged in a history book. Short and narrow, it wasn't big enough to be a desk or a dresser. One of its four thin legs ended in splinters where the tip of it had broken off. The bottoms of the other three legs were carved into fancy bird claws. There were holes where the handles to the two drawers underneath the table-top should have been, and its mirror was dull with black splotches and bordered by fancy curvy shapes carved in the wood.

"It's like a magic mirror," Ai said.

"Make a wish," Ben said.

They were both silent for a few seconds.

"I wish my family could see me," Ai whispered.

Ai's words sent an electric shock running right through Ben. She had whispered so softly, like she was talking to herself, but Ben had heard every word. He snuck a glance at her. Were they going through the same thing?

Ben and Ai were still staring at the furniture's rippled wood when the apartment door behind it opened. They both stumbled backward in surprise.

"We're sorry," a woman standing in the doorway said. Her hair was bright pink and fell in waves down to her shoulders. "We know your sign said recycling, but we have to get that out of here and we . . ."

She trailed off and rested her hands on her belly. It

was so large and round, it looked like she could have her baby tomorrow!

"It's okay," Ben said. It was small enough to fit on the dolly. "We can take it down."

"Appreciate it," another person said as they joined the woman in the doorway. They had hair that was shaved on the sides but wild on top. They had a pair of crutches and a cast all the way up to the knee.

"I'm Atom. With a *T*," they said, leaning on their crutches. "And this is Cypher." They pointed a crutch toward the pregnant woman.

"Between Atom's cast and the baby, we figured we could use some help," Cypher said. "I saw your sign and I thought maybe . . ."

"Don't worry. We got it. Plus . . ." Ai paused as she pulled her flyer out of her pocket. "My phone number is on here," she said. "Text us if you need any more help."

"Thank you," Atom said.

As they started testing the weight of the furniture, Atom leaned on the crutches and hopped around in a circle until they could work their way back into the apartment. Cypher waved and softly shut the door.

"Ready?" Ben said, gripping his side of the vanity.

"You didn't make your wish," Ai said.

"What?" Ben asked.

"Your wish," Ai said, pointing to the mirror.

Ben moved to stand in front of it. He snuck a glance at Ai out of the corner of his eye, then turned back to the mirror. All he could see when he looked in the mirror was his parents' angry faces. He suddenly felt the chill of their disagreements. He shivered.

"I wish my mom and my dad didn't hate each other. I wish we could be a family again." His voice was shaky, but he didn't whisper it.

"Oh," Ai said softly. "Things are bad at home?"

"Horrible," Ben said. "Ready?" He grabbed his end of the furniture.

Ai nodded. Together, they placed it on top of the flattened boxes on the dolly. As they pushed the dolly down the hall, Ben turned to Ai.

"What's wrong with your family?"

And for the first time in forever, Ai didn't look annoyed or confused. He didn't know why, but talking about their families felt like the most normal thing in the world. By the time they got down to the lobby, they didn't feel like competitors anymore; they felt like a team. Together, they navigated the dolly through the service entrance and across the sidewalk. After they put the furniture on the curb, they lingered there, looking at the deteriorating wood and splotchy mirror that had gotten them talking. Maybe it was a magic mirror after all. It didn't have the power to grant their wishes, but it helped them see that they didn't have to suffer their hard times all alone.

Secret Mission

Helping the neighbors made Liam feel good, but on a day like today, when his mind was drifting toward disaster, he didn't need to feel good. He needed to feel safe. So when he got the text to meet up to help in the building, he lied. He said he had to take care of his siblings, but the truth was his mother was off from work and Liam was free to spend the day doing what he wanted.

As soon as he climbed out of bed, he started packing his bag for a secret mission. When he had everything he needed, he put on his mask and gloves and left the apartment. He knew that his friends needed the elevators for the dolly, so he took the stairs. He knew that they always started on the top floor, so he headed downstairs, rushing past the floors his friends lived on. He planned to start on the fourth floor and he'd work his way down.

By the time he was done on the second floor, his friends would have finished with the top floors and he could sneak upstairs.

When he opened the door on the fourth floor, he looked to his left, then to his right. He wasn't doing anything wrong, but a secret mission had to be secret. He stepped out of the stairwell and walked quickly to the end of the hall. He stopped in front of the apartment that was farthest away from the elevator and pulled out his spray bottle and his paper towels. Then he sprayed the doorknob and wiped it clean with a paper towel.

After cleaning the second and third doorknobs, he realized his heart was thudding in his chest. When he was cleaning his fourth doorknob, his phone buzzed in his pocket. He jumped like he had been caught. The spray bottle slipped out of his hand and thudded to the floor. He laughed quietly to himself as he pulled out his phone. It was a text from Ai, asking what was taking Ben so long.

Putting his phone away, he moved on, falling into a rhythm as he cleaned, singing songs under his breath as he went from door to door. It was quick work—within minutes, he was back where he began. He quickly cleaned the doorknobs of the apartments near the elevator and the up and down buttons. He really wanted to call the elevator and wipe it down inside, but he didn't want to get caught.

He cleaned the stairwell instead. Switching to a fresh paper towel, he sprayed it with cleaning fluid and curved it around the handrails as he took the stairs down one flight. On the next floor, he was so confident that he was a danger to viruses everywhere that he decided he needed a superhero title. He spent his time cycling through possible names as he wiped down the doors on the next floor.

As he was finishing the third floor, he realized no one had seen him. He hadn't run into any friends or neighbors, and his mission was still secret. So he decided to call himself the Stealth Destroyer. No one could see him coming—he was as invisible as the germs themselves and he would wipe them out before they could hurt anybody.

On the next floor, he designed his costume as he worked. It would be light blue with a gold belt full of his antivirus supplies and gold wristbands with lasers that could kill germs in one shot. Halfway through cleaning the floor, he realized his costume needed one more thing: a cape, made out of a magical material that could make him invisible when he put it on.

He imagined flying all over the city, wiping down all the surfaces until they were so clean, they sparkled. He imagined the charts on the news would suddenly change direction. The numbers of sick people that had been going up would suddenly start going down as fewer and fewer people got sick. After he swept through the streets, there would be no more germs left to hurt people.

When he was sure his friends were done with the top floors, he pushed the up button on the elevator. As he waited, he wiped down the elevator doors and imagined his superhero self in action. He was deep in his fantasy with a goofy grin on his face when the elevator dinged and the doors slid open. Before he realized what was happening, something crashed into him and he fell to the floor.

"Sorry, man," he heard a voice say. "You alright?"

Liam grimaced and looked up. A man with spiky dark hair was looking down at him from a wheelchair. He had a huge face shield that covered him from his forehead to his chin with smooth clear plastic. A pile of boxes sat on his lap.

"I'm fine," he said. That wasn't exactly true. His leg was pounding where he had been hit, but he didn't want the guy to feel bad.

The guy reached out a gloved hand to Liam. "Let me help you up. What's your name?"

Liam reached up and took the man's hand, pulling against it until he was back on his feet.

"Liam," he said, limping slightly as he moved around the wheelchair to pick up three small packages that had scattered on the ground.

"Sorry, Liam," the guy said. "I'm Gene. You sure you're not hurt?"

Liam nodded and stacked the packages on top of the smaller ones on the guy's lap, then backed six feet away.

"I'll be fine."

"Good," Gene said, and turned his wheelchair away.

"Wait," Liam said. "Next time, me and my friends could help. We deliver packages and stuff."

"You think because I'm in a wheelchair I need your help?" Gene asked over his shoulder.

The guy's voice was suddenly so grouchy he may as well have said *back off.*

"Oh, no," Liam said. "We're helping everybody in the building. Old people and . . ."

Liam drifted off. He watched as the guy kept moving down the hall, passing two doors before swerving to face his apartment door.

"We do recycling too," Liam shouted.

"Got it, thanks," the man said, reaching into the pouch on the side of his wheelchair and pulling out his keys.

A strange feeling tickled him as the man disappeared into his apartment. He felt like he had just been split down the middle. One part of him knew exactly why Gene felt grouchy when Liam offered help. It was the exact same reason why Liam was cleaning doorknobs on his own. He wanted to do something to help himself and he wanted to do it on his own—without Ai feeling sorry for him, or Shayla pitching in to make him feel better, or Ben explaining how easy it was not to get caught up in anxiety. But the other part of him felt like his friends did, like he wanted to help make someone's life easier whether they wanted help or not.

He burst into a wide grin. Liam had helped without Gene knowing. For the moment at least, Gene had a germ-free doorknob, so there was one less chance that he would get the virus. *The Stealth Destroyer strikes again*, he thought. Still grinning, he punched the up button on the elevator, wiping down the doors as he waited. This time when he heard the elevator ding, he shook off his thoughts and stepped aside.

The super stepped off the elevator and looked at Liam in surprise.

"Your crew is on the tenth floor. What are you doing down here?"

Liam's mind buzzed. He thought about telling the super the truth. He wasn't doing anything wrong, but then he blurted, "I was just checking to see if there was any extra recycling left out."

"Uh-huh," the super said, and glanced down at Liam's bag. Liam thought about coming clean. It was a silly secret to keep, but the super didn't press him. He just said "See you" and walked on by.

The Power of Memory

After a few weeks living with Daisy, Shayla learned that there were pluses and minuses to owning a dog. There was the cuddling, but also the hair everywhere. There were the fun games, but also the nibbling on everything: furniture, plants, shoes. Shayla had also learned that Daisy was an excuse to leave the apartment, even if she had already spent hours with her friends. One busy afternoon, she timed Daisy's daily walk with Ai's and Liam's trip to the grocery store. Liam showed up with a brand-new gadget. It was a clear piece of plastic that covered his whole face. Without thinking, Shayla reached out and tipped it up. Liam made a loud sound that was hard to describe. It wasn't even words, just a growl that made Shayla snatch her hand back and apologize.

"It's for germs," Liam said, popping the face shield back in place. "To make sure they don't get in my eyes."

"Sorry," Shayla said. "I just wanted to see how it worked."

"I'll show you later. When we're inside," Liam said.

His words were short, but his voice wasn't so angry anymore.

"Let's spread out," Liam said, and pointed to where Shayla and Ai should stand. They walked all the way to the store that way—in a triangle shape, yelling so that everyone could hear one another along the way.

Shayla had learned that Daisy and the grocery store were not a good combination. Too many ankles to nip at and boxes to tip over. So while Ai and Liam shopped, Shayla strolled down the block so Daisy could continue sniffing at fences and chasing after tiny flying insects. She stopped short when she saw a new mural painted on the wall next to the barbershop. It was a huge painting of George Floyd, and crowded on the sidewalk in front of the mural was a cluster of flowers, candles, and handwritten notes. Her father had a photo album full of murals just like this one. The photos were from all across the country.

At least thirty of them were from before Shayla was born. He had started collecting them when he was a teenager but this was the first one she had seen in real life.

She was wondering how many more times this would happen when she felt Daisy pulling at the leash. She looked up to see Ai and Liam coming out of the store with a full cart of groceries.

"Did y'all get me a cinnamon roll?" Shayla asked, running up to them.

Ai rolled her eyes and waved a handful of envelopes in the air. "This money is the neighbors' money, it's not for treats." Each envelope had a name and an apartment number written on it. Shayla heard a rattling sound as Ai moved them around.

"Do you have change in there?"

"And a receipt. So they can know we're bringing the right change."

"The cashier must have loved you two," Shayla said. Just then she felt the leash slip out of her hand as Daisy jerked away and went racing down the block.

"Daisy!" Shayla yelled, and spun around to run after her. She could hear the wheels of the grocery cart squeaking behind her.

When Shayla was finally just a few feet away from

her, Daisy darted into a courtyard in the middle of the block.

"Daisy!" she yelled again, and stepped inside to search the courtyard.

She looked around, dodging a few prickly bushes and a black metal bench. Everywhere she looked there were trees, bushes, and flowers. She raced to the back of the courtyard just in time to see Daisy's tail disappear behind a row of tall leafy bushes.

At the edge of the bushes, she pushed the leaves out of the way and peeked into the narrow space between the bushes and the courtyard wall. She could see Daisy's tail just a few feet away.

"Come here, Daisy," she said, kneeling down and tugging Daisy's leash toward her.

Daisy struggled against the leash, but Shayla was stronger. When Daisy was within arm's reach, she scooped her up, then froze. Leaning forward, she saw the soles of a pair of boots. Taking a few steps closer, she gasped. The boots were attached to a person!

"Ai! Liam!" she yelled, scooting away as quickly as she could.

When Ai and Liam reached her, she pointed into the bushes and backed away with Daisy in her arms.

"What?" Liam said, peeking into the bushes. Shayla

heard a thunk as Liam's face shield hit against the wall.

"Look farther in," she said. "Look on the ground!"

"Is that . . . ?" Liam's voice faded.

"Let me see," Ai said, poking Liam in the back, but Liam didn't move.

"Are they okay?" Liam asked.

"Is who okay?" Ai yelled.

"There's somebody in there," Shayla said. She dumped Daisy into Ai's arms and dragged Liam away.

"Don't leave me!" she said, feeling braver now that her friends were there to back her up.

She flattened herself against the brick wall and started edging forward, letting the leaves tickle her face and arms. She leaned over the body, her legs tense, ready to run if the person looked dangerous.

"It's a woman," she yelled when she caught a glimpse of the person's face. The woman's eyes were closed and her black hair was spread out in the dirt.

"Is she breathing?" Ai yelled back.

Shayla reached out her foot and kicked one of the woman's boots. The boot jerked, but then went still again, pointing straight up, motionless.

"Is she breathing?" Ai yelled again.

"Give me a chance to check!" Shayla yelled back.

Shayla waited a few seconds to see if all the yelling would wake the woman up, but she still didn't wake up. She squinted, trying to see if her throat was moving, but there was a mask bunched around her neck and her BLACK LIVES MATTER T-shirt was too bulky for Shayla to see any motion in her chest.

Not knowing what else to do, Shayla squatted. She slowly poked the woman's leg with one finger. She yanked her finger back when she discovered the woman's leg was warm. Now that she knew the woman's body was warm, she lost her fear. Standing up, she used her foot to rock the woman back and forth, hoping to jiggle her awake. She pushed harder and harder until the woman finally stirred.

"She's waking up!" Shayla yelled, shuffling a few steps back.

The woman blinked a few times, then she leaned up on her elbow and rubbed her forehead. Her eyes were red and her face was streaked with dirt.

"Should we get her some water or something?" Liam yelled.

Shayla was silent as the woman started muttering, but her words were too choppy to understand. She almost pushed herself up to sitting, but then her eyes rolled back in her head and she fell back onto the dirt.

Shayla rushed back to her friends and described what happened.

"We should tell your dad," Liam said.

"No," Ai said, shaking her head. "We need my mom."

"But . . ." Shayla looked at Ai, searching for the right words. No one had seen Ai's mom since the beginning of the quarantine. Of course a nurse would be way better than her dad, but how did she think she was going to get her mother to leave her room?

A Crack of Light

All the way home, Ai thought about her interactions with her mother over the past few months. She was more like a delivery person or a nanny than a daughter. Her mother would take any food Ai had brought her. She'd let Ai brush her hair. Sometimes she was silent when Ai tried to talk to her. Other times she would give sleepy, whispered answers that were as empty as silence.

She paused in front of her parents' room. Her palms were sweaty and her stomach was starting to cramp. Before she could change her mind, she turned the doorknob and slowly pushed the door open. She went straight to the window and yanked the curtains open so that the sunlight came streaming in and chased the darkness out of the room. Then she turned to the bed. Her mother was in the middle of the bed, nothing more than a lump buried under the covers.

She took a deep breath and peeled back the blanket. Her mother flinched when the light hit her face, but she didn't open her eyes. For a few seconds, Ai just stood there, staring at what had become of her mother. Her mother loved beautiful clothes—and she would never start the day without brushing her hair until it was shiny and putting on plum-colored lipstick. She was nothing like this puffy-faced woman with tangled hair hiding under the sheets.

Remembering why she was there, Ai abruptly left the room and went to the kitchen to get a glass of water. In the bathroom, she collected her mother's hairbrush and lipstick. She placed everything on the bedside table, then pounced on the bed.

"Wake up, Mama," she said, shaking her mother's shoulder.

Her mother squeezed her eyes to shut them even tighter.

"Mama," she said. "Someone is hurt. You have to get up."

Her mother opened her eyes and lifted her head. There was a deep groove across her cheek where her face was pressed against the sheets.

"Kartika is hurt?" she whispered.

"No, Mama, a stranger," Ai replied. "A stranger is hurt."

Her mother laid her face back down on the bed and closed her eyes.

"Your father will help you," she said.

"He's at work," Ai said. "We need you."

Ai's mother fluttered her eyelids, but she didn't open her eyes again. Ai slid off the bed and picked up the glass of water from the bedside table.

"Mama, are you thirsty?" she asked. "I brought you water."

Ai's mother's hand shot out as she blindly felt in the air for the water.

"It's here, Mama," Ai said, holding the glass just out of her mother's reach.

She pushed herself up to sitting, but Ai held on to the glass, forcing her to scoot to the edge of the bed. As soon as her mom's feet touched the floor, Ai handed her the water and grabbed the brush. Brushing her mother's hair, Ai yanked out the tangles. A few times, she heard her mother's teeth clink against the glass as she jerked at her hair, but she didn't stop. While untangling her mother's hair, she launched into her story, describing the trip to the grocery store and the stranger they found.

"She's hurt, Mama," Ai said, wrapping up with

an explanation of how the woman's eyes rolled back in her head when she tried to sit up.

For a few seconds, her mother didn't speak. The only sound Ai could hear was the crackle of the brush moving through her mother's hair.

When there were no more tangles left, Ai held on to the brush, gripping it so hard her fingertips turned white under the pressure. Her mother reached past her and put the water glass back onto the bedside table with a thunk. Then she looked past Ai, her eyes darting back and forth. She cleared her throat.

"You found a woman unconscious in the bushes and you woke her up. She had trouble talking and she couldn't sit up?"

"Yes!" she said. Her heart leapt to hear her mother speaking in a normal voice after weeks of talking in whispers, but her excitement died when her mother didn't say anything else. She just sat there staring out into space.

"Mama," Ai said, touching her mother's shoulder. "What's wrong? Are you scared?"

"No, I'm not scared. I just . . ." Her mother broke off, shaking her head. Her eyes looked sad. "Sometimes life is a struggle."

"That's why we need you," Ai said. "This woman might really be hurt."

"Oh," her mother sighed. She seemed to snap out of her daze. She looked up at Ai and smoothed Ai's hair. "Of course I'll help."

Ai smiled and waited, but her mother still didn't move. She almost seemed as lost as the woman they had found in the courtyard. Ai looked around the room. The bedsheets were rumpled and the empty plate from last night's dinner was sitting on the chest at the foot of the bed. Everything in the room seemed to be waiting for an answer from her mom too.

"But do you feel strong enough to come outside and help?" Ai asked, squeezing her mom's hands.

"I'm sorry," her mom said with a sigh. Her eyes were wet.

"It's okay, Mama," Ai said.

"It's not okay," her mother said. "How long have I been in bed?"

Ai opened her mouth to answer, but then she decided to stay quiet. Whatever her mom was already feeling, she didn't want to make things worse.

"It doesn't matter, Mama. You're up now. Are you ready to get dressed?" She reached over to the bedside table, picked up her mother's lipstick, and held it out to her.

Even though it probably looked weird to her mother, Ai closed her eyes and prayed. *Please*, she said to herself. *Please let her say she feels better and she's going to help.* Her arm was aching from holding out the lipstick, but she refused to stop reaching toward her mother.

"You know, Ai," her mother said, hugging herself. "Sometimes life can be overwhelming. Promise me you'll talk to Ayah or Kartika if you . . ." She paused. Her eyes were still wet. ". . . especially if you can't talk to me."

Ai nodded, but she didn't move. Just when the ache in Ai's arm started to sharpen into pain, her mother heaved herself up off the bed and grabbed the lipstick. The touch of her mother's fingers sent a shock wave of joy through Ai's body. With a small sob, her mother pulled Ai toward her and gripped her in a tight hug. Holding on to her mother, Ai squeezed her eyes tight. She hoped getting her mother out of bed was the right thing to do. There was nothing but bad news outside her mother's bedroom, nothing out there to convince her mother that she should be awake for the rest of the quarantine. *Nothing good except me,*

Kartika, and Ayah, she thought to herself. She was sure getting her mother out of the apartment to help someone would make her mother feel strong, but a tiny bit of doubt echoed in the back of her mind. What if she was wrong? What if the safest place for her mother was right there at home?

Itching to Help

Ben didn't quite know what to do with himself. He had tagged along when Ai and Liam had brought Shayla's dad and Ai's mom to the courtyard. He thought it would be an adventure, but everyone was spread out around a row of bushes. Ben felt awkward. He wanted to figure out how to help, but he didn't have enough information to decide what to do. Then he saw Shayla playing with Daisy.

When he walked over to Shayla, she asked, "Did Liam tell you what happened?"

"Yeah. Is she bleeding?" Ben asked.

"Why? Are you gonna be sick?" Shayla shot back.

"No," Ben said, crossing his arms. "But no blood, right?"

"Nope. Nothing gross. She just looks like she hurt her head."

Ben knelt down and scratched behind Daisy's

ears. She wriggled around and Ben started laughing.

"I told you she could sleep over at your place some-times," Shayla said. "I know how much you love playing with her."

"I have to ask my parents," Ben said, patting Daisy's back.

"That's what you said last week," Shayla said.

Ben frowned. He wanted to explain why he was avoiding asking his parents, but he didn't think Shayla would understand. He couldn't imagine her dad screaming at her mom or slamming the furniture.

"So what are you and my dad doing here?" Shayla asked out of nowhere.

Ben scrunched his face up. "What?" he asked. He didn't try to hide the hurt sound in his voice. Why did it always feel like Shayla was trying to find a way to show that she didn't want him around?

"Sorry," she said. The she lowered her voice. "It's just that I didn't tell my dad I was coming to the store. I thought Liam and Ai were only bringing back her mom."

"Oh," Ben said. He felt a little embarrassed. Shayla wasn't trying to push him away; she was trying not to get in trouble with her dad.

Over by the bush, Liam was leaning on the wall staring into the gap, and Mr. Kwame was standing in front of the bushes looking over the top. Ai and Mrs. Utari were nowhere to be seen. Ben imagined them crouching over the woman, with tons of leaves hanging over their heads.

"An ambulance might take too long," Mr. Kwame said. "We might have to get her out ourselves."

"I don't think he's worried about where you were," Ben said. Then he laughed. "Doesn't it look like they're talking to the bush?"

Mrs. Utari came out from behind the bushes. She wiped her forehead. "She's weak and disoriented— and I think she needs to get checked out."

"Can we move her?" Mr. Kwame asked.

"No open wounds, nothing broken, and nothing seems to be wrong with her spine. She seems to have a pretty bad concussion, but she can probably walk with our help."

Ben went over to Liam and tugged at his arm.

"Let me see," Ben said.

Liam moved out of the way and Ben peeked behind the bushes. He saw Ai standing up and the woman lying at Ai's feet.

"I'll help," Ben said.

"What are you doing?" Ai whispered. "I'm helping my mom."

Ignoring Ai, Ben peeked over the bushes so that he could see the woman's face. Strands of her black hair were sticking to her forehead and her skin was pale and clammy.

Mrs. Utari clapped her hands. "You two—out of the way!"

"You're ruining everything," Ai hissed at Ben.

"What are you talking about? I just wanted to help!"

Ben walked away from the bushes and leaned on the wall.

"Liam," Mr. Kwame said. "Would it be okay if I borrowed your face shield? Just long enough for me to move her?"

Liam didn't answer. With a serious expression on his face, he removed his face shield, pulled a packet of wipes out of his pocket, and wiped it down.

As Liam handed Mr. Kwame the face shield, Ai came barreling out from behind the bushes. She crossed her arms and stared at Ben.

"What?" he said.

She looked over her shoulder to make sure no one else was listening.

"Do you remember what I told you about my mom?" she asked in a low voice. Her eyes narrowed as she questioned him.

He looked over his shoulder at Mrs. Utari. She was yelling instructions to Mr. Kwame as he worked to get the woman out from behind the bushes.

"This is the first time she's left the apartment in weeks. I want to spend time with her—and you're screwing it up!"

Ben's heart sank. He didn't want Ai to feel like he was competing with her again.

"I'm sorry," he said. "I only wanted to help."

"Fine," Ai whispered. "Just stay away from her."

They heard a rustling behind them, and they both turned to see Mr. Kwame helping the woman over to a bench. Everybody gathered in a half circle, spreading out around the bench.

"What's your name?" Mrs. Utari asked when the woman was settled on the bench.

The woman struggled to speak, but no words came out. She just made stammering and stuttering noises. After a short while, the sounds became frantic and frustrated.

Mrs. Utari squeezed the woman's leg. "It's okay, it's okay. It's totally normal for you to lose a little bit of memory while your head is healing. You need a brain scan. Do you understand?" Mrs. Utari paused.

When the woman nodded, Mrs. Utari said, "Okay, good. I am Nurse Utari and we're all going to work together to get you to a hospital, okay?"

Ben noticed Mrs. Utari was nodding a lot and talking in a singsong voice.

She reached into her pocket, then sighed. She pulled her hand out of her pocket. It was empty. "I don't have my phone."

"I'll call a car," Mr. Kwame said. "If we try to get an ambulance it'll take too long. We need a taxi."

Ben snuck a glance at Ai, but she wasn't paying any attention to him. She was busy staring intently at her mother, studying her as if she could learn something just by watching her movements. In that moment, it was like Ben knew exactly what Ai was feeling. Sometimes it felt like his parents were the whole world, like they were all that existed— and the fighting between them was all that there ever would be. But here was Ai, seeing the world in her mother. Ben looked around the courtyard. It wasn't just Ai; it seemed like everyone around him was desperate with their own worries. Yes, Ai was desperate for her mother to be okay, but Daisy desperately needed a home and Liam desperately wanted to stay safe. There was Shayla, desperate to win back Ai's friendship. And maybe this woman was the most terrified and desperate of them all—she probably wasn't worried about parents and friendship; she was probably just desperate to know her own name.

The World Turned
Inside Out

The first thing Liam did after Mr. Kwame gave him back his face shield was wipe it down and put it on, tugging at the strap to make sure it was securely in place. He had stayed out of the way while everyone else worked to get the woman out of the bushes, but now that she was sitting on the bench, Liam felt safe to approach her.

"She really can't remember her name?" Liam asked Ai.

Shayla smacked him on the arm. "Shhhh!" she said.

Liam snuck a glance at the woman. From the way her eyes crinkled and how her cheeks moved up, he could tell she was smiling. Her smile wasn't very big and it disappeared quickly, but it was unmistakable. It made Liam feel like she wouldn't mind talking.

"Maybe we can help," Liam said.

"How can we help?" Shayla asked.

Liam looked around the courtyard. There had to be a clue somewhere nearby that could explain how the woman got there. He looked up and saw the corner of a sheet flapping out of an open window overhead.

"Maybe you live here!" Liam said.

The woman looked around the courtyard, then she shook her head.

"I don't think so."

"What about your phone?" Shayla asked.

"Or your wallet?" Ben asked.

The woman leaned over to reach for her back pockets. She groaned. Her face tightened with pain as she slowly patted her back pockets, then the front ones. She shook her head again.

"Nothing," she said, spreading her fingers as if showing her empty palms for proof.

Everyone fell silent. For once there was no bickering and there were no jokes. In the quiet, Liam could feel everyone's worry. For a few seconds they all just sat there, looking in different directions, sharing the woman's sadness.

The woman broke the silence with a question.

"What street is that?"

She lifted her hand and pointed to the entrance of the courtyard. At the same time, she held her side, drawing her eyebrows together as if fighting the pain. Outside the courtyard, life was going on as usual, with people walking down the sidewalk and cars driving down the street.

"Rogers Street," Liam said. "Have you heard of it?"

In that moment, there was a loud clank, as if a truck had hit a bump in the street. One of the woman's arms went up to her head as if to protect it. She began blinking rapidly.

Shayla gasped.

"She's remembering," Ai said.

"Rogers Street," the woman mumbled.

"So you know this street?" Liam asked.

"I was here," she said. She let out a gasp that sounded a bit like a sob. "With lots of people. We were screaming. No." She shook her head. "We were chanting. But when we got to the corner, something stopped us and we were all squeezed together."

She fell silent for a few seconds, and her eyes moved back and forth. Liam imagined she was seeing an explosion of images in her head.

"She was at the protest," Shayla whispered.

"Shhhh," Liam said sharply.

The woman took a deep breath and started talking again.

"I can see it. It was a wall of police that stopped us, but everything else is a blur. There was pushing and shoving. I heard a loud crack. Tear gas maybe. Everyone started running. I got pushed to the ground. Some people stepped on me. I felt a pair of hands help me up. Then I was alone again. Something hit me on the head and I followed a bunch of people here. My head was hurting so bad. I just had to lie down."

Everyone was quiet again, but this time it wasn't because they didn't know what to say. Liam could see that everyone was thinking. He could almost see the questions piling up in their minds.

Ai jumped up suddenly.

"I'm going to tell my mom," she said.

After she left, the woman just sat there with her shoulders hunched and her hands clenched, rocking back and forth. Liam recognized those movements. He made them sometimes when he was trying to keep his mind under control.

Liam plucked a worry stone out of his pocket, took a step closer to the woman, and handed it to her.

Her eyebrows lifted up in surprise.

"It's a worry stone," Liam said.

Shayla and Ben kept quiet while the woman examined the stone.

"Hold it with the dip up and run your thumb back and forth across the dip."

The woman flipped the stone over, then dropped her hand into her lap. She slowly started moving her thumb back and forth over the stone. When he noticed she had started a rhythm, Liam nodded and backed away.

When she leaned back against the bench, he smiled. For a few seconds, Liam felt like a superhero again. He never thought the thing that made him feel so weak at times could also make him feel strong. But today, he saw how all the things he knew about his problems could help someone else.

Mr. Kwame approached the bench. "Mrs. Utari will get you to the hospital," he said to the woman. "She's just calling a car and will be back to walk you out as soon as it gets here."

The woman nodded silently, her thumb still moving across the worry stone.

"Kids," he said. "We're rolling out." Before turning away, he pressed his hands together and gave the woman a slight bow. "I hope you get better soon."

Then he motioned for everyone to follow him.

As everyone followed Mr. Kwame, Mrs. Utari returned to the courtyard. With her face full of worry, Ai wrapped her mom in a hug. Liam was struck by a familiar feeling. He knew how it felt to be a kid trying to take care of your mom.

After Ai waved goodbye to her mother and joined everyone else on the sidewalk, Liam tried to figure out the best way for them to keep their distance from one another while walking home.

"Dad?" Shayla said, interrupting Liam's thoughts.

"Yep?"

"She said she was at a protest and the cops came and broke it up. Did you hear about it?"

Mr. Kwame nodded. "Yes, it happened right around the corner."

"On our block?" Ben asked.

Mr. Kwame paused and put his hands on his hips. All the kids stopped walking while he stood there, quietly thinking.

"It happened one block over. I was going to check it out on my run later. But I suppose we could take the long way home and check it out together."

"I want to see," Ai said.

"You sure?" Mr. Kwame asked.

Everyone nodded, except Liam. He wasn't sure if he wanted to see it, but Mr. Kwame had already tipped one foot back, spun around, and pointed in the opposite direction.

"Reroute," he yelled.

As they all giggled, everyone tried to do their best spin to change direction. They moved down the block in a wiggling mess of arms and legs as everyone took turns showing off flashy dance moves. After a while, Liam got into the fun, moving with stiff arms and legs like a robot as they made their way down the block.

When they got to the corner, all movement stopped. They stood there, looking around them at the damaged buildings with their mouths hanging open in shock. All up and down the block, it looked like a tornado had swept through. Piles of glass glittered on the concrete beneath smashed store windows. Bent doorframes. Boxes scattered on the ground. Two posts were bent over, their signs swinging upside down. All along the way, there was graffiti scrawled on the walls.

"The protest we saw didn't look anything like this," Shayla said.

All Liam could think about was what it would take to put everything back together again.

"This hurts to look at," Mr. Kwame said, and started walking again.

The friends started walking, glass crunching under their feet. The sidewalk was full of little obstacles— random pieces of metal, mysterious canisters, and masks on the ground. Everywhere they turned, they saw trash and debris.

"Who did this, Mr. Kwame?" Liam asked.

Mr. Kwame sighed and rubbed his forehead.

"I think you deserve ice pops after the morning you've had. Why don't we go back to the building to get a treat—and we can talk about everything," he said, motioning to the mess. "And if any parents complain, just tell them it's American history."

He kicked a spray can out of the way and started walking again. Everyone followed along, dragging their feet as they moved past the destruction on the street.

A Horrible History

"Alright, everybody. All those funky, dirty hands need to get washed," Mr. Kwame said.

While everyone took turns washing their hands, he wiped down the door handle, his keys, and his cell phone.

When everyone got back, he pointed to four chairs he had spread around the room.

"Take a seat. Masks off just to eat the ice pops. When you start talking—even if you are still eating—put your mask on. Everyone keeps their germs to themselves. Deal?"

As Shayla handed out ice pops, her dad disappeared to wash his hands. After she brought the box back to the freezer and settled on the windowsill next to his sewing machine, he came back and sat in his sewing seat with a heavy sigh.

Shayla drew in a breath. She hoped he wouldn't

fuss at her for meeting her friends at the grocery store without telling him.

"Liam, you asked who did that outside—who destroyed the street? Have you ever seen this quote?"

He pointed to the wall above the sofa. Liam twisted around. There, on a white piece of paper in black letters, was a small sign that said A RIOT IS THE LANGUAGE OF THE UNHEARD. —MARTIN LUTHER KING, JR.

"There was a riot in our neighborhood last night?" Ai asked.

"Well, I'm sure that's not what they planned. There are all kinds of people taking advantage of the protests to be violent."

"And to steal," Shayla chimed in, thinking about the boxes scattered on the sidewalk.

Her dad nodded.

"So, it's not the protesters?" Ben asked. "My dad said they would be better off if they didn't destroy their own neighborhood."

Shayla whipped her head around to her dad quickly to check his reaction. There were certain things that people could say that made her father really angry. Focusing on broken and stolen things rather than murdered people was a quick way to make him upset.

"It's easy to think that way," her dad said.

Shayla let out her breath, happy to hear his voice was still calm.

"We all wish there was an easy and polite way to protect our rights. But no, it's not true that the protesters would be better off. Do you know how we know that?" he asked.

Shayla looked around the room. Between licks of their ice pops, her friends shook their heads.

"Because it's been going on a long time," Shayla burst out.

"You're good at math, right?" Shayla's dad asked Ben.

Ben shrugged and put his mask on. "Research," he said.

"He does like numbers though," Liam said after tugging his mask over his mouth.

"Well, how many years do you think it should take to stop police from killing innocent unarmed people?" Shayla's dad asked.

"Zero years," Ben said. "Killing innocent people is just wrong."

"Well, innocent Black people have been killed repeatedly in this country for over four hundred years."

"Four hundred years!" Liam said. "That's a long time."

Mr. Kwame nodded. "I went to protests with my

parents. That was thirty years ago. My parents protested their whole lives. Their parents tried to fight it too. When you add up all the years, you start to understand the frustration."

"But why?" Ben asked. "Why are Black people treated differently?"

Shayla saw her dad turn around and look at her. She knew he was trying to decide exactly how much to say to them. Right within arm's reach, he had a cabinet filled with newspaper clippings, books, pamphlets, and albums full of photographs and papers, all about the violence that Black people had survived. When he opened his history cabinet, there was no telling what he might pull out. He had shown her pictures of lynchings—when Black people were murdered for looking a White person in the eye, for trying to buy land, for being in the wrong neighborhood. The pictures were frightening, with White families all around—men pointing, women smiling with their children, while a dead person hung from a tree. He had pictures of police dogs and water hoses turned on protesters. He even had pictures of enslaved Black people during the earliest times of American history, their bodies marked by missing hands and scars across their backs, some even had their heads stuck on poles.

"They do it because they can," he said, looking back at her friends. "Have you heard of a social contract?"

They all shook their heads. Shayla fought not to roll her eyes. When her father got going, it was impossible to make him stop.

"The social contract is the idea that we, the people of this country, accept the rules and laws that define our government. It's like how traffic lights work. As a society, we agree to stop at lights and go at green. What would happen if we didn't?"

"Chaos," Ai said.

"Death," Ben shouted out.

"Right," Shayla's dad said. "The laws are words on a piece of paper and the social contract is what makes them real. So when police officers kill innocent Black people and nobody complains and the police officers keep their jobs, what do you think the social contract is saying?"

"That it's okay to kill Black people," Liam said.

Shayla's dad nodded.

"And you know who makes the social contract?"

"Who?" Liam asked.

"You," her father said, standing up. Then he pointed to Ben and Ai and said, "And you. And you."

"How?" Ben asked. His voice sounded a little angry,

like he thought Shayla's dad was blaming him.

"By what you decide to do when people are treated unfairly. Do you ignore it or do you speak up?"

"So we have to speak up," Ai said.

"And sometimes, when you've been speaking up for years, you have to act up," Shayla's dad said.

"So that's why they put graffiti on the buildings?" Liam asked.

"And broke the glass?" Ben added.

Shayla's dad waved his hand in the air. "That's a distraction. There's people who don't believe in rules, people who just want free stuff, there's people who just want to break things, people who don't believe Black people are being treated unfairly. All those people are showing up at the protests, but they are a distraction. They're not the point. The point is we have a big problem and we all have to focus on using our voices in the best way we can."

"So will you take us to a protest?" Shayla asked, looking at her dad hopefully.

"Girl," her dad said. "I can't trust y'all to stay safe in this building. Why would I trust you at a protest?"

"I know how to act at a protest," she shot back.

"Okay, well, show me," he said. "Show me what

you'll do if the police harass you at a protest."

"What?" Shayla asked. She suddenly regretted jumping into the conversation.

"Show them what you tell the cops if they stop you."

Shayla shook her head. Her face suddenly felt hot. "I don't want to," she said.

"You think I should trust you to do it in public, but you're afraid to show your friends what you know? Show them."

When her father sat down and crossed his arms, she knew that the conversation was over. He leaned back in his seat and waited for her to do what he asked.

Shayla put her shoulders back and stared straight ahead. She was afraid that if she looked at her friends, she wouldn't go through with it. She put her hands up in the air and took a big breath.

"My name is Shayla Marks. I am a child," she said. "I am unarmed. I am following your directions. Please do not shoot."

Her voice trembled at the end, the way it never did when she was doing it just for her dad. When she was done, the room was completely silent. She slunk back against the window frame and stared down at the toes of her socks. It felt wrong that her friends had seen her like that. She didn't want them to look at her differently, like she wasn't herself anymore, like she was something strange or an alien. Not a kid like them.

Without another word, Shayla's dad stood up and started walking out of the room.

"Daddy?" Shayla said.

As soon as he turned back to face her, she saw the emotion on his face. Every time he tried to teach her about being Black in America, he ended up caught between feeling proud of how much she had learned and heartbroken that he had to teach her about this horrible history.

"But what are we supposed to do?" Ai asked.

"If I had the answer, if I knew how to protect my child . . ." Her father's voice started to shake. He broke off and abruptly walked out of the room.

"So how are we going to help Black people?" Ben asked as soon as Mr. Kwame was gone.

"No!" Shayla yelled.

They all swiveled around to look at Shayla in surprise.

"Sorry," she said. "I didn't mean to yell. My dad would be so mad if he thought you were doing it to help us."

Ben looked at her, completely confused. "But we *are* doing it to help you."

"We don't want you to get hurt by the police," Liam said.

"My dad said things won't change until people start protesting for themselves," Shayla said.

"Not for Black people," Ai said to herself softly.

"Do it for yourself," Shayla said. "That's what my dad would say. Do you want to live in a world where it's okay for me to be murdered?"

Everyone shook their head. Liam stared at her with sad eyes, Ben's eyes looked frightened, and Ai's eyes were burning with rage.

"So we have to do it for the world we want to live in. Or we'll never have a fair world."

After a few seconds of letting it sink in, Ai waved her stick from her ice pop in the air and said, "Enough thinking. Let's make a plan. What are we going to do to fight?"

Best and Worst Morning Ever

Ai woke up with a gasp. In her dream, she was trapped facedown, like George Floyd, with a man kneeling on her legs, another man kneeling on her back, and someone else kneeling on her neck. She twisted and turned, thrashing as hard as she could to get them off her, but it didn't work. Her breath got tight. She started gasping for air, and when she felt like she couldn't take one more breath, she woke up. Her heart was pounding hard and she was shaking with terror. "You're alive," she told herself. "It was a dream."

Out of nowhere, an image of Shayla with her hands up flashed in her mind. Ai's chest got tight again. This time, not in fear for her life, but for Shayla's. Then Shayla's words echoed in her mind: *Don't do it for me. Do it for yourself. Do it for the world you want to live in.*

The next face that flashed in her mind was Trennell's. He had an expression on his face that was like a mixture of anger and sadness. She could hear the sound of Ms. Breaux's voice yelling at him like she always did when he wasn't paying attention in class. Then in a flash, she saw Ms. Breaux leaning over to Megan and Gemma, softly asking them to stop talking and do their work.

Ai sat up abruptly. It was just like Mr. Kwame said. They all saw it happening and they all knew it was wrong, but they didn't say anything. Was it all connected to how George Floyd died? And now that she knew how dangerous it was, would she be brave enough to stand up and say something the next time she saw it happening? She decided she would try.

The smell of food interrupted her thoughts. She inhaled deeply. That smell was congee and there was only one person in the apartment who cooked congee. She swung her legs out of bed and slid her feet into her slippers. Her mom was in the kitchen cooking everyone's favorite breakfast!

She rushed through brushing her teeth and cleaning her face, then raced to the kitchen. Her mother wrapped her in a hug and kissed the top of her head. Her mom's hair was messy but not tangled. Her face was a little puffy, but her eyes were bright and shining.

"Come to help?" she asked. She pointed to the cabinet on the other side of the kitchen, then tapped Ai on the nose. "Could you get the bowls?"

Ai nodded, her mind whirling as she searched the cabinet for bowls. What did it mean that her mother was standing here making breakfast? Was she done hiding in her room?

"Mama?" she said hesitantly.

"Ai?" her mom said back.

Ai was silent as she lined up four bowls on the counter.

"Are you going to stay out of your room now?" she finally asked.

Her mom reached out and rubbed Ai's back. "Yes, I am going to try to stay out of my room." Ai squinted her eyes. She noticed that her mother hadn't said she would stay out of her room, she said she would try—and she paused before she said it, like *try* was the most important word of the sentence.

Ai smiled as her mother returned to the stove to check the pots. As soon as her mother's back was turned, Ai dropped the smile from her face. She ran her finger around the rims of the empty bowls. Her mother was the strongest person she knew. If she wanted to stay out of her room, Ai didn't understand why she couldn't do it.

"But," she said, looking up at her mother's back. "Do you feel like you are *ready* to stay out of your room?"

Copying her mother, she made *ready* heavier than all the other words. Her mother brought a steaming pot over to the counter. She looked at Ai before dipping a ladle into the pot.

"Ai, you know that everyone has brain chemicals that influence their moods, right?" her mother said as she started filling the bowls with congee.

Ai nodded. Her mother had explained this to her many times.

"Yes," Ai said. "And your chemicals are low sometimes and you get depressed, but . . ."

Ai fell silent. Her mother grabbed the congee pot and went back to the stove.

"But . . ." Ai said, plunging back in as soon as her mother returned to the counter with a pan of chicken. "Last time you said I could trust you. I could trust that if you got too depressed you would go see your doctor and you would check your medicine."

"That's exactly what I did, honey. When I went to the hospital last week, I spoke to my doctor. That's why I'm standing here talking to you."

Ai's mind did a little loop. She could force her mother to explain why she waited so long to go to the doctor—or she could focus on the fact that her mother was getting better.

"So, you feel better?" she asked.

"A little," her mother said. "I need to keep working with myself and my therapist. And the medicine needs time to work too."

She put the chicken back on the stove and returned with a chopping board covered with sliced scallions.

"So you're still . . ."

Her mother rested the chopping board down next to the bowls.

"I'm still struggling, but I'm in a better place."

"Does that mean you're taking your medicine?"

She paused and looked at Ai. They stared into each other's eyes, the hot breakfast bowls steaming between them. She reached out and squeezed Ai's arm.

"This isn't fair to you—it isn't fair to any of you."

Ai squeezed her hands together and tried to make sure her voice was strong.

"It's not your fault if you're depressed, Mama, but you promised if you get too depressed you would go see your doctor."

Ai's mother folded her hands and looked down at them. Then she looked up at Ai.

"There's certain promises I can't make," she said. "I can't promise I won't need to spend some time in my room. I can't promise I'm going to be in the kitchen every day. But I can promise that I won't let it go that long again."

Ai's heart soared. It wasn't a magical promise, that everything would be perfect, but Ai wasn't a baby anymore. She didn't need magic—she needed her mother. And if her mother promised to fight, she believed her.

Her mother broke into a grin when she saw the relief on Ai's face.

"Do you feel better now?"

Ai nodded.

"Good. Now can you get the shrimp crackers?"

Ai skipped to the pantry, grabbed the crackers, and brought them to the counter. She looked over the bowls. Each one was perfect. The chicken was neatly stacked on one side, and the scallions were scattered on the other. There was a blank third of the bowl, a stretch of congee that wasn't covered by anything. That's where she placed the shrimp crackers. Then she rubbed her hands together. Breakfast was going to be delicious!

"Kartikaaaaaaaaaaaaaa!" Ai yelled.

Ai's mother tapped her arm. "Don't yell. Go get her."

When Ai opened the door to Kartika's room, all thoughts of breakfast disappeared from her mind. She just stood there in the doorway, frozen, as Kartika hung over the side of her bed, coughing so hard her whole body shook. When the coughing spell passed, Kartika looked up and locked eyes with Ai. Her face was covered with sweat.

"Mama!" Ai yelled.

Her mother took one look at Kartika and nudged Ai away.

"Go call your father," she said.

She ran to her parents' bedroom and shook her dad awake.

"Ayah, Ayah! Kartika's sick," she said.

Her father opened his eyes and rubbed his face.

"What?" he asked groggily.

"Kartika. She's coughing. Mama said to get you."

Her father sat up. "And what's that sound? Is the doorbell ringing?"

Ai listened for a few seconds and heard the doorbell ring. She took her father's hands and pulled him up from the bed.

"I'll answer the door. You go check on Kartika."

Her father nodded and stumbled out of the bedroom. Ai grabbed a mask from the closet and rushed to the front door. Cracking it open, she peeked out.

Shayla, Liam, and Ben were standing there. They each had a stack of flyers in their hands.

Ai groaned. They had all spent days texting one another about their research and nights working on flyers for their new, secret project, but between her mother and Kartika, Ai had forgotten all about their plans.

"I can't come," Ai said sharply.

"What? We can't go without you!" Shayla said.

"What about your flyers?" Ben asked.

"I'll get them for you, but you have to go without me."

Ai rushed to her room and got the flyers she had spent all night finishing. Swinging the door open, she darted out, placed them in a stack on the floor, then ducked back into the apartment.

The door slammed shut behind her.

"Ai, what's wrong?" Shayla yelled from outside the apartment.

Ai peeked through the peephole and saw that Shayla's eyebrows were tense with confusion.

"My mom's better, but now Kartika's sick. I just need to stay home."

"Is it . . ."

"We don't know yet," Ai said, cutting Liam off before he could ask if it was COVID.

Outside, the group fell silent. Ai felt a little dizzy. She was hungry, but she had lost her appetite. Now she had to send her friends off on their new mission without her.

"Text me later and tell me how it goes," Ai said, doing everything she could to make her voice sound cheerful, to convince herself and her friends that there was nothing to worry about.

How to Talk about a Broken World

When they stepped out of the elevator, Shayla flipped her messenger bag open and pulled out a bright red shoebox.

"I'm ready," she said.

"What is that?" Ben asked. He crossed his arms. They had spent a week planning what they were going to do and Shayla had never once mentioned a box.

"It's a pledge box." Shayla flipped the box around and showed Ben and Liam the big black letters that said PLEDGE on the other side.

"Like Mr. Bloomfeld's?" Liam asked.

Their principal, Mr. Bloomfeld, had a huge

wooden pledge box in his office. Every month he handed out a different pledge and the whole school filled it out. They pledged to save electricity and to be good members of the school community, to welcome new students and to do their best on their homework.

Shayla pulled a stack of papers out of her bag. They said STOP RACISM PLEDGE across the top. "After you and Liam talk to people about your flyers, I'm going to ask them to take a pledge," she said.

"But that's going to take so long!" Ben burst out. He fell silent while his mind flipped through calculations. "It could take us an hour and a half to get through one floor! Besides, you never said anything about a pledge box when we were planning."

"For your information," Shayla said, emphasizing all the syllables in the word *information*, "I don't tell you all my ideas."

Liam held his hands up.

"Please don't start," he said. "It sucks that Ai can't come, but we can't start fighting. We have to act like a team."

Ben opened his mouth to say, *Teams share information*, but then he thought about Kartika and fell silent.

He quietly followed Liam and Shayla down the hall. He had been so close to starting a big fight with Shayla, but when Liam mentioned Ai, Ben suddenly realized Shayla and her pledge box weren't the problem. The problem was that he was worried about Kartika. Whenever he worried, he got antsy—and when he got antsy, he got grouchy. And changing a plan on him when he was already grouchy was an easy way to get him mad.

"So let's do this," Liam said, and walked away without saying another word.

By the time Ben and Shayla caught up with him, he had already knocked on the door and whoever was inside was already at the door. When Ben saw Cypher standing in the doorway, he waved.

"Hi! How is Atom's leg?"

"They still need crutches but their leg is slowly healing," she said, and rested her hands on her belly. It hadn't been that long since he and Ai had moved their furniture, but her belly looked way bigger. "I see some new faces here, but somebody's missing?"

"Ai," Ben said. "She's . . . she's . . ." Ben looked a little lost.

"She's not feeling well," Shayla said, jumping in.

"Oh, I hope she feels better," Cypher said.

"So, we're here to talk about a problem in our world," Liam said, cutting into the conversation.

Ben's stomach tensed a little knowing what Liam was going to say.

"Okay," Cypher said with a nod.

"Have you heard of Tamir Rice?" Liam asked.

Cypher shook her head. Liam handed her one of the flyers he'd made.

"He's a twelve-year-old boy who was killed by the police for playing with a toy gun in a park."

"Wow," Cypher said.

"When the policeman arrived, he shot Tamir two seconds after he got out of his car," Liam continued.

"That doesn't seem right," Cypher said, frowning.

Ben sighed softly. So far everything was going well.

"You probably know about George Floyd, but there's so many innocent Black people who were killed by police," Shayla said. "We learned that one reason why it keeps happening is because people don't speak up about it. So we're making a building pledge to talk about it and fight racism."

Cypher looked down at her belly and looked back at the kids.

"I agree with you, but I can't do any protesting right now."

"Racism is everywhere!" Ben blurted out. He didn't feel so comfortable trying to convince someone to sign a pledge, but he felt very comfortable with facts.

Cypher jerked her head toward Ben as if his outburst surprised her.

"I suppose that's true," she said.

"So, this pledge just says you will speak up if you see racism happening," Shayla said, handing Cypher the paper.

Cypher took the paper. She kept one hand on her belly while she read the pledge. After a few seconds, Ben realized he was holding his breath. Telling the neighbors about racism was harder than asking them if they needed help. Plus, having a pledge made it more complicated.

"There was something that happened last week that bothered me," Cypher said, looking up from the paper. "At the drugstore, when I was leaving, I walked through a metal detector at the same time as a Black man and it went off. The security guard stopped him and checked his bags, but he didn't stop me."

When Ben heard that, he reached for his back pocket where he usually kept his notebook, but his pocket was empty. In Ben's brain, stories always turned into data, and hearing Cypher's story made him want to start a chart.

"What did you do?" Shayla asked softly.

Cypher shook her head sadly. "I didn't do anything. It bothered me in the moment, but then I forgot about it. I should have said something. Do you have a pen?"

Shayla reached into her bag and handed Cypher one of the pens they'd sterilized.

Ben watched as she leaned the paper on the wall and wrote in the blank space under the pledge, then signed her name.

"Thanks!" Liam said.

Cypher smiled, waved at them, and closed the door.

"She signed it!" Shayla whooped, then she did a little hop.

"On to the next one," Liam said, and started walking to the next apartment.

Ben had barely said a word to Cypher, so he charged ahead to catch up with Liam. He didn't get a chance to knock on the door, but when it opened, he was right by Liam's side.

"Oh," Ben said softly in surprise when he saw the man in the doorway was in a wheelchair. Then he took a deep breath and plowed into his speech.

"Have you heard of Oscar Grant?" he asked.

The man looked a little startled.

"I'm sorry, Mr. Gene," Liam said. "We're here to talk about an important issue in our community."

Mr. Gene nodded. He didn't speak, so Ben couldn't tell if he was friendly or not, so he kept talking.

"Oscar Grant was handcuffed in a train station and while he was lying on the ground the police shot him in the back and killed him."

Mr. Gene still didn't say anything, but Ben could tell he was listening. He handed the flyer he'd made about Oscar Grant to Mr. Gene. For a few seconds, they were all quiet. Ben and Liam were holding their flyers while Mr. Gene sat there staring at them, patiently waiting.

Shayla broke the silence, rescuing Ben.

"We're collecting pledges in the building to help fight racism," she said, handing Mr. Gene the pledge.

"What does my pledge have to do with Oscar Grant?" Mr. Gene asked, and he stared at all three of them like he was challenging them.

"If we don't talk about unfairness and racism, people will keep getting killed," Ben said.

"And Black people can't be the only ones fighting it," Shayla said. "We can only change it if everyone as a community agrees that it's wrong."

"You know," Mr. Gene said. He paused and reached up to adjust his glasses, and Ben saw the flash of his black fingernails. "Black people aren't the only ones who are murdered by the police."

"No?" Liam said.

"No," Mr. Gene said, shaking his head. "People with mental differences and disabilities are frequently killed by the police too."

"Like Elijah McClain!" Shayla said.

"Who?" Ben asked. He had remembered all the people they had researched. They had never talked about Elijah McClain.

"Yes, exactly," Mr. Gene said.

Shayla crossed her arms. "But he was Black too," she said.

Ben looked back and forth between Shayla and Mr. Gene. He felt an explosion of chaotic and disorganized thoughts. Learning about all the people who had been killed by the police was scary, but it had given Ben some order in his mind. It made him feel like he could understand the problem and do something about it, but now he felt like his mind was trapped again. There were too many stories, and it felt like he'd never learn them all.

Shayla knew so much more about the problem than he did. Looking at her standing there with her arms crossed, Ben felt like he was living life protected from this horrible knowledge and she was standing right in the middle of the storm. He felt conflicted and overwhelmed, but he decided he would fix that when they were done. There was only one way he ever tackled a problem: with observation and research. He would go home and study more.

"Are you going to sign it?" he snapped at Mr. Gene.

"Of course I am," Mr. Gene said, pulling a pen out of his shirt pocket. "I just wanted you to know that many different kinds of people are dying and need our help."

When Mr. Gene gave Shayla his pledge, Ben turned and walked away without another word. He circled back and grabbed a pledge sheet from Shayla's hand. Then as Shayla and Liam said goodbye to Mr. Gene, he leaned on a wall in the middle of the hallway and filled out the pledge sheet. On the blank lines under *I Pledge To*, he wrote, "Learn more about racism and share what I learn with everyone I meet." Then he handed it back to Shayla and led the way to the next apartment.

The Balance Point

The first thing Liam saw when he woke up was the pile of flyers stacked on the floor. When Ai had roped him into helping the neighbors, he had no idea it would turn into a big project like this. People were really listening to them, and with all the protests going on, it felt like they were doing something important.

Suddenly, Liam's eyes popped open. He realized he hadn't heard from Ai since the day she told them Kartika was sick. He grabbed his phone and started to type.

Liam

Is Kartika okay?

Liam rolled onto his stomach and waited for Ai to text back. Finally, his phone buzzed.

Ai

She tested positive.

But the rest of us don't have it.

You got tested?

Did it hurt?

Everything he had read about the test sounded horrible.

Ai

It burned.

But it was fast.

Liam

I hope Kartika gets better soon.

As he typed, he heard a crashing sound come from his sisters' room.

"Owww," one of them yelled.

He dropped his phone on the bed, threw off his covers, and rushed out of his bedroom. In a blur of toys and teasing, tickles and screaming, he managed to get the twins dressed and fed before texting Shayla to tell her that he was heading to the grocery store earlier than planned. By the time he wrestled the twins into their shoes and put on his face shield, his gloves, and his mask, Shayla had texted back saying she would meet him in the lobby.

When they got downstairs, Cara and Cayla were delighted to discover that Daisy was with Shayla.

Liam was excited to see that Mr. Kwame was going to the store with them. On the way to the store, he told Mr. Kwame all about the conversations they had with the neighbors. Liam's heart felt warm when Mr. Kwame said he was proud of them.

Liam felt proud of himself for other reasons. In the early part of the quarantine, going to the grocery store was terrifying. But now he felt safe behind his face shield and with his hands protected by gloves. While Liam and Shayla shopped, Mr. Kwame took over with Cara and Cayla, walking them up and down the block. Liam was so comfortable in the store that instead of getting antsy, he laughed at Shayla when she made the cashier wait while she organized everyone's money into the correct envelopes.

"Ha-ha," Shayla said. "Wait until it's your turn. Ai makes it look so easy, but it's not."

When Liam and Shayla pushed the cart out of the store, they noticed Mr. Kwame deep in conversation with Mrs. Q from the corner store. Today, her hijab and long dress were a deep purple and she held a bag of bread in her hand. The twins ran up to her with their hands outstretched, jumping up and down. She gave them each a slice of bread and they ran a few feet, ripping the bread into chunks and throwing them in the air, squealing as pigeons gathered and fought over the food.

"So you think it's going to be a few weeks?" Mr. Kwame asked Mrs. Q as Liam and Shayla joined them.

"At least that," Mrs. Q said with a shrug. "With COVID, nobody has the supplies they need."

"Hello!" she said. "It's nice to see you two."

"Nice to see you too," Liam and Shayla said at the same time.

Usually, when Liam told an adult it was nice to see them, he was just being polite. But with Mrs. Q he really meant it. She was always cheerful when they went in her store after school for treats, she never complained when they paid for drinks with a handful of coins, and every Halloween she gave away the best candy.

"Did something happen to the store?" Shayla said.

"The front window was shattered and a few shelves were broken," Mrs. Q said, waving her hand toward the end of the block.

Liam and Shayla walked over to the curb to look down the block. On the opposite corner about a half block away, they could see boarded-up windows at Mrs. Q's store and broken glass on the sidewalk. That explained what Mrs. Q was doing there. Liam had never seen her outside. She was always behind the counter of her corner store.

Liam and Shayla returned to Mrs. Q.

"Did the protesters do that?" Liam asked.

Mrs. Q shook her head and shrugged like it was nothing. "We don't know who did it."

"But aren't you mad at them?" Shayla asked.

"I'm not happy about it." Mrs. Q sighed. "But it's a building. I have insurance. We'll fix it. It's not a life."

After spending the morning feeling like he was helping, Liam felt a little sad. How could he be proud when Mrs. Q's store was destroyed?

"I'm sorry, Mrs. Q," Shayla said.

Mrs. Q shook her hands. "No, no, no. We will be okay," she said. "This happens in my country too. We want everything to look nice, but underneath, things are not nice."

"But people can't just break things!" Liam said, his voice pitching up.

"It's hard to argue about what people should and shouldn't do when everyone is messing up," Mr. Kwame said.

Mrs. Q held her hand flat in front of Liam and Shayla.

"This is life," she said. "Impossible to balance. Sometimes it tilts this way." She tipped her hand to the right. "But then it hurts too many people, so we push it back that way. But then that upsets too many people, so they push it back this way. You'll see, as you get older. It's like a roller coaster, up and down. We keep going back and forth like that. We're never going to get perfectly balanced, but we have to keep pushing to make sure we get as close as possible to fairness."

Liam held his head. "That makes me dizzy."

Mrs. Q laughed. "Me too," she said. "But these kinds of explosions are everywhere. It's bigger than my little shop. Things will get back into balance."

"I hope things get into a better balance," Mr. Kwame said. "I don't want to go back to all this death being normal."

As Mrs. Q nodded. Then she said, "I have to go, but when I get back in my shop, drinks are on me!"

Then she waved goodbye and everyone shifted around. Shayla took Daisy's leash, Liam grabbed Cara's and Cayla's hands, and Mr. Kwame pushed the cart from Shayla.

On the walk home, Liam felt a familiar anxiety nibbling at his mind. It wasn't as strong as panic and it wasn't attached to anything particular, but he couldn't pretend his mood hadn't changed. He felt a heaviness whispering around him, so he focused on holding on to Cara's and Cayla's hands as they started to skip.

His mind wandered back to what Mrs. Q said about life swinging in more than one direction. It reminded him of something his therapist was always saying. She said a panic attack is like getting stuck in one thought, one big disaster bubble, but life was never one thing and everything changes.

Bobbing up and down, Liam remembered all the little things that had changed because of everything he and his friends were doing in the building. Then he thought how he wasn't the only person who got stuck sometimes. Liam got stuck in his mind, but right now, Ai was stuck in the apartment—again.

Instead of staying stuck in his sadness about Mrs. Q's shop, he decided he would do a little thing for Ai—just to show her how much of a difference they had all made while she was in quarantine.

Giving and Getting

"Shayla, are you listening?" Ben asked. His voice got louder, breaking into Shayla's thoughts.

"I'm listening!" she said, her mind scrambling to remember what Ben had said. Instead of paying attention to what they were doing, Shayla's mind had been wandering. She was thinking about what Mrs. Q said about the world being out of balance. From that thought, she started imagining the world was a machine with stuck parts. If it were a toy she could hold in her hands, she could tinker with it and figure out how to get it moving smoothly again, but the world was way too big for one set of hands to fix.

"Sorry," Shayla said. "I wasn't listening. What did you say?"

"I said 'no more flyers,'" Ben said, showing his empty hands.

Shayla had only one more left. The elevator dinged and they stepped off on the second floor.

"Let's give out this one, then get more from Ai," Shayla said.

Without discussing it, Shayla and Ben drifted to Mr. Grove's door.

When they got there, they could hear wild jazz playing inside. After they rang the doorbell, Shayla started humming with the music, and Ben started tapping his foot. When Mr. Grove opened the door, they were making loud sounds along with the music. They stopped singing instantly and started laughing with embarrassment.

"Oh no," Mr. Grove said. "Don't let me stop you. Scatting is good for the brain cells." Then he started making his own sounds: "Do-bee-do-wop-wahhhh."

When Mr. Grove sang with them, their embarrassment disappeared. The song ended, and Shayla handed Mr. Grove her flyer.

"This is—" she said.

Mr. Grove cut her off before she could explain.

"I know who this is," he said. "What's this? A school project?"

Ben shook his head. "We wanted to do something about George Floyd, but we can't go to the protests."

"And not just George Floyd," Shayla said. "For everybody who was killed." Then she pointed to her chest. "For me."

"And for me," Ben said, jumping in. "We all have to speak up so this can stop happening."

Mr. Grove looked at them proudly. "I always say it," he said. "Old folks are too set in their ways. I always say we gotta wait for the right young ones to be born so they can make this world make sense."

Shayla snuck a look at Ben. She knew they were doing the pledge to help change things, but if all the things people tried in the past didn't change things, why did he think their flyers would work?

"But do you really think we can change things?" Shayla asked. "Do you think this will really help?"

"That's the mystery, isn't it?" Mr. Grove said. "Can't tell you how many years of my life I spent trying to help fix this mess. Let me tell you, people have tried every which way. We had lawsuits and boycotts, we had protests and voting drives, we even had self-defense groups. A lot of people died trying to figure this all out." Mr. Grove got quiet and gazed over their heads with a faraway look in his eye.

"That's what I mean, Mr. Grove. If all that didn't work, how's a little piece of paper supposed to help?"

"Did you know," Mr. Grove said, "water can cut into stone?"

Shayla looked over at Ben with a confused expression on her face.

"You mean, like, over time?" Ben asked. "Like dripping onto something for years?"

"That's exactly what I mean. You all keep taking action and see how much stone you can wear through."

Sometimes Mr. Grove talked in plain language and sometimes he talked in riddles. Shayla knew that when he was in a riddling mood, there was no point in trying to get him to start talking straight. She looked over at Ben and he was staring up at the ceiling.

"What are you doing?" she asked.

"Calculating how long it takes for water to cut a hole in stone," Ben said.

Shayla shook her head. Only Ben would try to figure out something like that.

"Thanks, Mr. Grove," she said.

"Keep going, young ones!" he said, and softly closed his door.

●●●

When they got to Ai's floor, they were surprised to see a colorful pile of boxes, bags, and bottles in front of her door.

"Oh my god!" Shayla said, rushing to the door.

Digging through the pile, they found cards, flowers, aspirin, gloves, masks, and a few boxes of tissues.

"We dropped some of this stuff off with the groceries!" Shayla said, ringing the doorbell.

When Ai's dad answered the door, they both stepped back. First he saw Shayla and Ben, then he saw all the gifts in front of his door.

"You two did this?" he asked, his eyes wide with surprise.

Shayla shook her head. "No," she said. "It was the neighbors."

Then for a few seconds, the three of them stood there in silence, marveling at how the kindness they'd given had somehow found its way back.

●●●

Shayla leaned on the gate next to their building and silently ate her ice pop. She didn't offer Ben one and she didn't bring Daisy downstairs. She wanted to be alone to think. As she enjoyed the sweet, icy treat, she thought about how small she felt and how big the problems of the world were. The virus, racism, even the climate—when she thought about how dangerous and frightening everything was, it was hard to feel proud of the things the Quartet was doing.

She finished her ice pop with a sigh and headed back to the building. When she was opening the front door, a woman stopped her.

"Is this 360 Rogers Street?" she asked.

Shayla nodded.

"Does . . ." She paused, reached into her bag, and pulled out a business card. Shayla squinted at her long, curly hair and the hospital bracelet on her wrist. "Does Eli Utari live here?"

Shayla let go of the door and it slammed shut.

"You're the one we found," she said.

"You're the one who found me?" The woman pitched forward with her arms outstretched like she wanted to hug Shayla, then she stopped and took a few steps backward. "Thank you so much!" she said, clasping her hands together.

"So you're okay?" Shayla asked.

The woman shrugged. "I know my name and I remember where I live, but I'm in cognitive behavioral therapy, physical therapy, and occupational therapy . . . It doesn't matter. I just wanted to thank you and your friends. Who knows what would have happened if you didn't find me."

Shayla felt her heart warm. No matter how big the problems of the world were, this was something they had done—and she was sure it made a difference.

"I want to thank Mrs. Utari too. Is she here?"

"Probably, but you can't see her. She's in quarantine."

The woman sagged, her chest caving in like the news was a physical punch. She fanned herself, her hand waving in the air and her eyes darting back and forth like she had lost her memory all over again.

Shayla held out her hands to calm the woman. "She's fine. She's just quarantining for safety," she said. She didn't mention Kartika.

The woman pressed her hands on her head, then she squatted down and opened her bag. She pulled out six colorful bags and put them on the ground in front of Shayla.

"Can you . . ." The woman paused. She stood up and clasped her hands. "Can you share these with everyone else? I just wanted to thank you all for help-ing me."

She covered her face with her hands for a few sec-onds, then she backed away.

"Thanks," Shayla said, and scooped up the bags. She gave the woman a wave and watched her turn and walk away.

She stepped into the building, pausing when her

phone buzzed. She shifted the bags to her wrists and checked her phone.

Liam

I have an idea. Meet me in the courtyard tomorrow after class.

Between the gifts for Ai and the visit from the woman they had helped, the day was already full of surprises. She smiled. At a time when she was full of doubt, she was excited to have a surprise to look forward to.

Separated, But Still Together

Stuck in her apartment, Ai tried not to be sad about all the things the Quartet was doing without her. When she had started, helping out in the building turned into an excuse to escape the silence at home. Now that her home wasn't as silent anymore, she realized that helping the neighbors was her new normal—and she missed it.

She received all the texts from the neighbors and made all the schedules, but it wasn't the same as actually helping out, so she started a new project. Every morning of quarantine, she cut out colorful shapes until her fingers got tired. One day, she would cut out green shapes, the next day, she cut out orange. She cut until she had gone through a whole pack of construction paper, then she had to decide what to do with the pile of shapes.

One evening, she carried the stack of shapes to her closet and started taping them to the closet door. She didn't have a plan, so she just let the colors guide her. Sometimes she clustered one color together. Sometimes she mixed up the colors. When she had covered the whole door, she stepped back to look at the patterns. She was shocked to see that from far away, her paper collage looked like a huge painting or a mural.

She was taking a picture of her artwork to send to her grandparents in Indonesia when the doorbell rang. She raced out of her room to answer it, but her father got there first. By the time she got to the door, he was already closing it.

"Was it Shayla? Did someone bring the mail or more stuff for Kartika?" she asked. Every time her friends came with gifts from the neighbors, it reminded her of how much fun they had together and how much the neighbors appreciated them.

He shook his head and pointed to the living room.

"It was Liam. He said we should look out the window."

"The window?" Ai asked, grabbing her father's hand as they made their way down the hall.

In the living room, Ai pushed past her father. In

her rush to get to the window, she brushed past the wooden puppet hanging off the corner of the bookshelf.

"Careful!" her father yelled as the puppet's limbs clattered against the bookshelf. "Whatever they want you to see will still be there when you get to the window."

"Sorry," she shrieked as she leaned on the window-sill and pulled the window open.

Looking down below, Ai searched the courtyard for Liam, but it was empty.

But then she heard someone scream her name. It was Shayla, standing at the far end of the courtyard, waving up at her.

"Shayla!" Ai yelled, and waved back.

"Look!" Shayla pointed to the wall.

Ai saw small white squares of paper stuck to one of the courtyard walls. It reminded her of the collage that she had just finished on her closet door.

"What is it?" she screamed.

Shayla took out her phone and pointed to it. Ai saw Shayla taking pictures of the papers on the wall and Ai went to her room to grab her phone. Opening her text messages, she saw that Shayla had sent her six photos of papers that said STOP RACISM PLEDGE across the top. Each paper had a different name and apartment number on it. She called Shayla.

"It's all the pledges?" she asked when Shayla answered the phone.

"Thirty of them!" Shayla said. Then she put the phone down and yelled, "It's time, Ben!"

Within a few seconds, a bright blue square of light appeared on the blank wall across from Ai's window.

Shayla put her thumbs up. "Everybody ready?" she yelled.

"Who are you talking to?" Ai asked.

Shayla pointed to the windows. Looking around, Ai searched all the windows that faced the courtyard and shrieked in surprise. Most of the windows had people in them. Ai recognized some of them by the shape of their shadows. She could see Mr. Grove's Afro and Cypher's big round belly. Looking closer, she saw Mrs. Romulus was in her window too. Mrs. Romulus waved at her. Seeing the neighbors she hadn't been able to help since Kartika got sick filled her with joy.

"Ayah, come see," she said, motioning for her dad to join her.

She pointed out all the neighbors she recognized and told him how the Quartet had helped them.

"You ready?" Shayla asked, interrupting her.

In her excitement, Ai had forgotten that they were on the phone.

"There's more?" she asked.

"You'll see; just hang up," Shayla said. She clicked her phone off and she pointed to one of the apartments above Ai's head. The blue square on the wall blinked, then it turned black. After a few seconds, the big colorful titles of a movie showed up, projected on the wall from the apartment above her.

Ai gasped. "Should we tell Mama?"

"We should let her rest," her father said, hugging Ai.

Ai leaned against her dad and smiled. Just a few minutes ago, she had been alone in her room, keeping herself busy as best she could. Now here she was, watching a movie with the whole building! As the movie began, Ai looked around at the windows again. In the dark, it was hard to tell who was doing what, but she caught glimpses of pets and plants behind the neighbors as they looked out their windows to enjoy the movie.

She pulled away from her father and stepped away from the window.

"What? Ai? You're not going to watch?" her father asked.

"I'll be right back."

In her room, she rummaged through her art drawer until she found her charcoal pencils. Then she grabbed her large drawing pad, returned to the living room, and turned to a fresh page.

"Ah," her father said when he saw her making the first few strokes on the blank page. "Inspiration has struck."

Just then, everyone erupted in laughter. She looked up just in time to see a cartoon porcupine struggling to pull an explosion of cupcakes off his quills. Ai and her father glanced at each other, then joined the rest of the building in laughter.

As the porcupine and his friends—a hippo and an antelope—got into sticky situations and close escapes, Ai kept an eye on the cartoon escapades as she sketched the people and shapes that came into her mind. She dedicated a special section of her page to her family. As she drew, tears sprang to her eyes. Not because she was sad or scared, but because she was relieved. In just the past week, so much had changed. Her mother had come out of her room, her father seemed less distant, and Kartika was coughing less and sitting up more. Everything could have turned out so much worse.

There was another explosion of laughter and Ai looked up just in time to see the animal friends clinging to a wooden raft that was tumbling down a waterfall. As she laughed along with her neighbors, she felt her shoulders relax. With her father holding her close, she let go of all the tension and worry she had been holding on to. Seeing her father watch the movie, eyes wide open with surprise, mouth turned up in laughter, she thought he probably needed to laugh as much as she did.

She tightened her grip on her charcoal pencil. With the laughter surrounding her and her father near, she realized that all their struggles didn't just make her feel sad; they also made her feel proud. In hard times, they didn't break down—they got stronger. In that moment, she was sure that what she had told Liam in Mr. O's classroom closet at the beginning of all this was true. Together, as a family and as a community, they were all going to be okay.

The Changing World

When Ai finally got out of quarantine, it felt like a celebration. Ignoring the schedule, the Quartet decided they would all go to the grocery store together. On the way there, everyone talked over one another as they caught Ai up on everything that had happened with the neighbors while she was stuck at home. It was hard to believe that when this all started, whenever the four of them were thrown together, they had nothing to share but stubborn silences and awkward glances. But now everything around them had changed—and they had changed too.

When they turned the corner onto the block of the grocery store, they heard the faraway sound of chanting voices.

"A protest!" Ai said.

"Just for you," Shayla said.

"We should join in!" Ben said.

"No, we shouldn't," Shayla said. "My dad finally let me leave the apartment without him. I'm not about to mess that up."

"We have to do something!" Liam said.

Shayla turned to Liam in surprise. "You, Liam? You want us to break the rules?"

"We have to do something. Don't we?" Liam said. "After everything we've been doing in the building."

"Let's just get the groceries," Ben said as they neared the entrance to the grocery store.

At the door, Ai threw her hands up. "I know what we can do!"

"What?" Shayla asked.

"You'll see," Ai said, and led the way into the grocery store.

●●●

The Quartet stood on the corner looking at the stream of protesters flowing past them. As they watched row after row of people walking alongside one another and chanting together, it was easy to see that none of the people looked exactly the same. There were tall people and short people, young people and old. Some had spiky hair, some had fuzzy hair, some had no hair. There were masks and signs with all kinds of messages. For a while, the Quartet just stood there reading the signs as the protesters marched by.

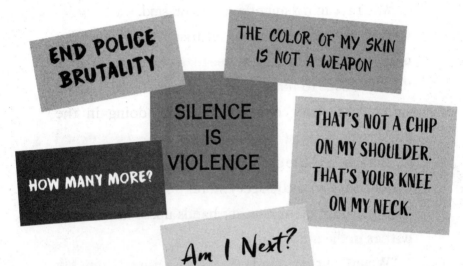

"Are we going to do this?" Ben asked.

Liam moved away from the protesters and stood behind the cart.

"I'll hand it to you and you all can hand it out. Like an assembly line," he said. He broke open the plastic packaging holding together a tray of water bottles.

Ai reached her gloved hand out and Liam handed her two bottles of water. She turned and stepped off the curb.

"Water!" she yelled at the people passing. She waved both the bottles in the air. "Water!"

A hand reached out and Ai gave them a water bottle without getting a good look at their face. A few seconds later, another hand reached out and Ai gave them the second bottle.

"That was easy," she said, clapping her hands. Her eyes were shining with excitement as she stepped back up onto the curb.

Both Shayla and Ben got two bottles each. Together, they stepped off the curb and started waving the bottles in the air.

"Water!" they yelled. The water quickly disappeared.

For the next hour, the Quartet went back and forth between the cart and the street, scrambling to give away all three trays of water.

When all the water was gone, Ai said, "Let's go buy more!"

Liam shook his head. "Can't. I have to finish my social studies project."

Shayla groaned. "I have to finish mine too."

"What about you?" Ben asked Ai.

"I started it, but I'm not done."

"Me neither," said Ben.

Shayla gasped dramatically. "Not you two. Ms. Breaux's favorites. Are you slacking?"

"Shut up," Ai said, laughing.

"How about this?" Shayla said as she grabbed the cart and wheeled it around. "Whoever finishes the project first sends it to the rest of us."

Ben got a funny look on his face. "That's cheating," he said.

"How's it cheating?" Shayla asked. "It's a personal timeline and a family interview. How is anybody going to cheat off you?"

"I'll send mine, and you can send me yours," Liam said. "I might need the motivation."

"Good. What about you two?" Shayla asked, looking at Ai and Ben. "Is it a deal?"

"Deal," they said.

Then they walked home, talking about everything they had seen at the protest all the way back to the building.

●●●

Even though he said he needed motivation, Liam was the first one to send his project. It came while Ai was helping her mom cook dinner, Shayla was helping her dad cut out masks, and Ben was cleaning out Bucky's cage. His timeline was typed in neat boxes and it focused on his anxiety about the virus, what he learned by cleaning the building, and the masks and gloves that made him feel safe.

As soon as Ben received Liam's project, he started working on his. When he sent it, Liam was watching Cayla and Cara splash in the tub, Ai was washing the dishes, and Shayla was eating dinner. Ben's timeline focused on numbers: the number of neighbors they helped, the number of people who got sick from the virus, the number of states that had protests.

Ai sent hers in while Liam was welcoming his mom home from work, Ben was playing a board game with his parents, and Shayla was procrastinating on getting started on her project. Ai's timeline was all about her close calls with the virus—discovering Mrs. Connor, finding the woman in the courtyard, and Kartika getting sick.

After Shayla read everyone else's interviews and timelines, she picked up the phone to call her mother. It took her five minutes to explain the project and tell her mom what her friends had written about. Then she took notes while they talked about her mother's childhood, the coronavirus, and the protests. Thinking about how sad and tired her father was, Shayla asked her mom if she thought things would change because of the protests. Her mom sighed.

"Progress is tricky," she said. "Things are changing all the time, but you can't always feel them changing, so you just have to commit to the fight."

"But what if it's really hard? Or if you think you're helping but you're just not doing enough?" Shayla asked.

"You still have to try," her mom said. "Life's not about getting exactly what you want when you want it. It's about growing stronger and fighting for the things that matter to you. As long as you do that and you use your voice for good, things will change."

"But what about you and Daddy? All those marches you went to when you were in college and nothing changed."

"The change is now, sweetheart," her mom said. "We don't get to decide when or how our actions make a difference, we can just do our best. We thought we could change things when we were marching, but it turns out we were just showing the next generation how to do it. Now you're going to pick up the fight and make it stick."

"Me?" Shayla asked.

"You, and Ben, and Ai, and Liam. And all the kids your age. You are going to change the world."

"But we're too young," Shayla said. "We can't even protest."

Her mom laughed.

"Look at what you're doing in the building. You've already started!"

"But that's not changing the world. We just talked to the neighbors."

"How do you think you change the world, Shayla?" her mom asked.

Even though her mother couldn't see her, Shayla shrugged her shoulders.

"You change the world one person at a time."

"So you really think handing out pieces of paper in the building can change the world?" Shayla asked.

"That's the beauty of changing the world," her mom said. "You are the world—we all are. So when we change our communities, we change the world."

Shayla fell into silence, thinking about what her mother had said. When Shayla didn't say anything else, her mom said, "Okay, sweetheart, I know it's late there. Do you have enough for your project?"

"Yep," Shayla said.

"Talk next week," her mom said.

"Yep," Shayla said again.

"I love you and I'm proud of you, honey," her mom said.

"Thank you, Mom," Shayla said. "I love you too." Then she clicked the phone off and turned to a fresh page in her notebook.

Shayla's pen hovered over the paper as she tried to figure out how to start writing. Turning to look out the window, she could see a few lights twinkling. They were just tiny lights in a sea of darkness, but they burned bright. Staring into the night, she felt like one of those tiny lights swimming in the darkness.

She sat there thinking about everything her mother had told her and all that had happened since the world turned upside down. Just like the darkness, life could overwhelm her, but she was learning that being small didn't mean she didn't matter. Even if she was just one tiny speck on the planet, she could be like one of those tiny lights burning so brightly in the night sky. She was starting to believe that if she kept fighting for the things she loved, her voice could be heard. If she was brave and always stayed true to herself, she too could burn bright.

ACKNOWLEDGMENTS

This book was inspired by all the unique ways that people managed life in the quarantine—and by the new conversations that are erupting around social justice in communities around the world. I wrote it in nine months! Here's how.

April: When the quarantine started, I joined a writing group (Altered Fluid), a creativity group (Creative Quarantine), art meet-ups with my sisters and cousins, and yoga meet-ups with friends. In the middle of all this creativity, I decided I needed to write a new book. *I thank my creative community for holding me up during the isolation of quarantine and helping me focus on what matters most to me: my creativity.* **In April, I wrote the outline for the book.**

May: In May, my job announced it was downsizing my division. A week later, George Floyd was murdered. I broke down in tears during a meeting with my coleaders. We were dismantling my department and I was mourning the death of a man. *I thank my coleaders for meeting me where I was and supporting me in my grief.* **In May, I wrote the first seven chapters and revised the outline to include social justice issues.**

June: I had lots of conversations with my editor and she showed outlines and early pages to lots of people at her job. After an early enthusiastic response, I polished the pages. *I thank my editor for her partnership and cheerleading throughout the process.* **In June, I revised the first seven chapters.**

July: When Scholastic decided to publish the book, my agent and editor got busy negotiating the contract. *I thank my agent for her expertise, persistence, and guidance.* **In July, I wrote the first half of the book.**

August: In art making, I have discovered if you judge your work at its early stages, you may never complete it, so I decided my first draft would not be perfect. *I am so grateful for what art teaches me and for the mental fortitude to let the process be messy!* **In August, I completed the first draft of the book!**

September: According to my parents, the book was already written the moment I decided to write it. They are my biggest cheerleaders. My father called me early in the quarantine one day and told me I was a success exactly as I was. He had evidence and backup points. *I thank both my parents for always seeing and celebrating my power and my talent.* **In September, I fleshed out plot and character dynamics based on feedback from my editor.**

November: Telling four different plot lines with four different personal challenges wasn't easy. When thinking about how kids could commit to anti-racism, I referenced two books. *I thank Tiffany Jewell for* This Book Is Anti-Racist *and Anastasia Higginbotham for* Not My Idea. *I am grateful for everyone who is using their talents to make our society better.* **In November, I turned in the revised draft of the book.**

December: Finding the best way to say something, cutting out repetition, enhancing themes—the writing work I live for. My daughter watched over me the entire time I was writing. She made sure I ate, rested, and stayed hydrated. *I thank her for being the best quarantine roomie I could ever have.* **I finished the book in December and turned in the final draft on January 8, 2021!**

"Books are labors of love—dreams that only come alive through you, the reader." —K. Ibura